i. AMENABLE
ii. SITUATIONSHIP
iii. MAMA (MOTHER)

By PINEL MOTSWAGOLE

AMENABLE!!

First edition. March 30, 2023.

ISBN: 978-0620960076

Written by Pinel Motswagole.

Table of Contents

Pinel Motswagole 065 828 7194

AMENABLE!

1. Dictionary

Data from Oxford Languages[1]

amen·able

[əˈmiːnəb(ə)l]

ADJECTIVE

amenable (adjective)

1. open and responsive to suggestion; easily persuaded or controlled:

"parents who have amenable children"

synonyms

compliant[2] · acquiescent[3] · biddable[4] · manageable[5] · controllable[6] · governable[7] · persuadable[8] · tractable[9] ·

---

1. https://www.bing.com/ck/
   a?!&&p=653842f29231f206JmltdHM9MTY4MDA0ODAwMCZpZD0yYWVlOWFmOC1jOTU5LTYwODEtMzliMS04ODg0YzgyYjYxYTAmaW5zaWQ9NTU5MQ&ptn=3&hsh=3&fclid=2aee9af8-c959-6081-39b1-8884c82b61a0&psq=amenable+synonym&cu=a1aHR0cDovL3d3dy5veGZvcmRkaWN0aW9uYXJpZXMuY29tLw&ntb=1

2. https://www.bing.com/ck/
   a?!&&p=b1785472963404c9JmltdHM9MTY4MDA0ODAwMCZpZD0yYWVlOWFmOC1jOTU5LTYwODEtMzliMS04ODg0YzgyYjYxYTAmaW5zaWQ9NTU5OA&ptn=3&hsh=3&fclid=2aee9af8-c959-6081-39b1-8884c82b61a0&u=a1L3NlYXJjaD9xPWRlZmluZStjb21wbGlhbnQmRk9STT1EQ1RSSVVk&ntb=1

3. https://www.bing.com/ck/
   a?!&&p=6e5fd079b8dcdd8dJmltdHM9MTY4MDA0ODAwMCZpZ3VpZD0yYWVlOWFm
   OC1jOTU5LTYwODEtMzliMS04ODg0YzgyYjYxYTAmaW5zaWQ9NTU5OQ&ptn=3&hsh
   =3&fclid=2aee9af8-c959-6081-39b1-
   8884c82b61a0&u=a1L3NlYXJjaD9xPWRlZmluZSthY3F1aWVzY2VudCZGT1JNPURDVFJR
   WQ&ntb=1

4. https://www.bing.com/ck/
   a?!&&p=80193c474b1de521JmltdHM9MTY4MDA0ODAwMCZpZ3VpZD0yYWVlOWFm
   OC1jOTU5LTYwODEtMzliMS04ODg0YzgyYjYxYTAmaW5zaWQ9NTYwMA&ptn=3&hsh=
   3&fclid=2aee9af8-c959-6081-39b1-
   8884c82b61a0&u=a1L3NlYXJjaD9xPWRlZmluZStiaWRkYWJsZSZGT1JNPURDVFJRWQ
   &ntb=1

5. https://www.bing.com/ck/
   a?!&&p=0102f4a4e8456108JmltdHM9MTY4MDA0ODAwMCZpZ3VpZD0yYWVlOWFmO
   C1jOTU5LTYwODEtMzliMS04ODg0YzgyYjYxYTAmaW5zaWQ9NTYwMQ&ptn=3&hsh=3
   &fclid=2aee9af8-c959-6081-39b1-
   8884c82b61a0&u=a1L3NlYXJjaD9xPWRlZmluZSttYW5hZ2VhYmxlJkZPUk09RENUUlFZ
   &ntb=1

6. https://www.bing.com/ck/
   a?!&&p=28553be6097051f2JmltdHM9MTY4MDA0ODAwMCZpZ3VpZD0yYWVlOWFm
   OC1jOTU5LTYwODEtMzliMS04ODg0YzgyYjYxYTAmaW5zaWQ9NTYwMg&ptn=3&hsh=
   3&fclid=2aee9af8-c959-6081-39b1-
   8884c82b61a0&u=a1L3NlYXJjaD9xPWRlZmluZStjb250cm9sbGFibGUmRk9STT1EQ1RSU
   Vk&ntb=1

7. https://www.bing.com/ck/
   a?!&&p=aa674280123bc6efJmltdHM9MTY4MDA0ODAwMCZpZ3VpZD0yYWVlOWFmO
   C1jOTU5LTYwODEtMzliMS04ODg0YzgyYjYxYTAmaW5zaWQ9NTYwMw&ptn=3&hsh=3
   &fclid=2aee9af8-c959-6081-39b1-
   8884c82b61a0&u=a1L3NlYXJjaD9xPWRlZmluZStnb3Zlcm5hYmxlJkZPUk09RENUUlFZ&n
   tb=1

8. https://www.bing.com/ck/
   a?!&&p=f619319d4793cdfeJmltdHM9MTY4MDA0ODAwMCZpZ3VpZD0yYWVlOWFmO

C1jOTU5LTYwODEtMzliMS04ODg0YzgyYjYxYTAmaW5zaWQ9NTYwNA&ptn=3&hsh=3
&fclid=2aee9af8-c959-6081-39b1-
8884c82b61a0&u=a1L3NlYXJjaD9xPWRlZmluZStwZXJzdWFkYWJsZSZGT1JNPURDVFJ
RWQ&ntb=1

9. https://www.bing.com/ck/
a?!&&p=aea0613a377cab85JmltdHM9MTY4MDA0ODAwMCZpZ3VpZD0yYWVlOWFmO
C1jOTU5LTYwODEtMzliMS04ODg0YzgyYjYxYTAmaW5zaWQ9NTYwNQ&ptn=3&hsh=3
&fclid=2aee9af8-c959-6081-39b1-
8884c82b61a0&u=a1L3NlYXJjaD9xPWRlZmluZSt0cmFjdGFibGUmUmRk9STT1EQ1RSUVk&
ntb=1

responsive[10] · pliant[11] · flexible[12] · malleable[13] · complaisant[14] · accommodating[15] · docile[16] · submissive[17] · obedient[18] · tame[19]

10. https://www.bing.com/ck/

a?!&&p=e346a596c8eaf2d1JmltdHM9MTY4MDA0ODAwMCZpZ3VpZD0yYWVlOWFmOC1jOTU5LTYwODEtMzliMS04ODg0YzgyYjYxYTAmaW5zaWQ9NTYwNg&ptn=3&hsh=3&fclid=2aee9af8-c959-6081-39b1-8884c82b61a0&u=a1L3NlYXJjaD9xPWRlZmluZStyZXNwb25zaXZlIjkZPUk09RENUUlFZ&ntb=1

11. https://www.bing.com/ck/

a?!&&p=2a5afacc9e72b381JmltdHM9MTY4MDA0ODAwMCZpZ3VpZD0yYWVlOWFmOC1jOTU5LTYwODEtMzliMS04ODg0YzgyYjYxYTAmaW5zaWQ9NTYwNw&ptn=3&hsh=3&fclid=2aee9af8-c959-6081-39b1-8884c82b61a0&u=a1L3NlYXJjaD9xPWRlZmluZStwbGlhbnQmRk9TT1EQ1RSUVk&ntb=1

12. https://www.bing.com/ck/

a?!&&p=da3d04128a310720JmltdHM9MTY4MDA0ODAwMCZpZ3VpZD0yYWVlOWFmOC1jOTU5LTYwODEtMzliMS04ODg0YzgyYjYxYTAmaW5zaWQ9NTYwOA&ptn=3&hsh=3&fclid=2aee9af8-c959-6081-39b1-8884c82b61a0&u=a1L3NlYXJjaD9xPWRlZmluZStmbGV4aWJsZSZGT1JNPURDVFJRWQ&ntb=1

13. https://www.bing.com/ck/

a?!&&p=fdaa977390ed6666JmltdHM9MTY4MDA0ODAwMCZpZ3VpZD0yYWVlOWFmOC1jOTU5LTYwODEtMzliMS04ODg0YzgyYjYxYTAmaW5zaWQ9NTYwOQ&ptn=3&hsh=3&fclid=2aee9af8-c959-6081-39b1-8884c82b61a0&u=a1L3NlYXJjaD9xPWRlZmluZSttYWxsZWFibGUmRk9STT1EQ1RSUVk&ntb=1

14. https://www.bing.com/ck/

a?!&&p=7eca501a5ba2aeb1JmltdHM9MTY4MDA0ODAwMCZpZ3VpZD0yYWVlOWFmOC1jOTU5LTYwODEtMzliMS04ODg0YzgyYjYxYTAmaW5zaWQ9NTYxMA&ptn=3&hsh=3&fclid=2aee9af8-c959-6081-39b1-8884c82b61a0&u=a1L3NlYXJjaD9xPWRlZmluZStjb21wbGFpc2FudCZGT1JNPURDVFJRWQ&ntb=1

15. https://www.bing.com/ck/
a?!&&p=b3f1e51736971519JmltdHM9MTY4MDA0ODAwMCZpZ3VpZD0yYWVlOWFm
OC1jOTU5LTYwODEtMzliMS04ODg0YzgyYjYxYTAmaW5zaWQ9NTYxMQ&ptn=3&hsh=
3&fclid=2aee9af8-c959-6081-39b1-
8884c82b61a0&u=a1L3NlYXJjaD9xPWRlZmluZSthY2NvbW1vZGF0aW5nJkZPUk09RENU
UlFZ&ntb=1

16. https://www.bing.com/ck/
a?!&&p=ed5a7221b18e5582JmltdHM9MTY4MDA0ODAwMCZpZ3VpZD0yYWVlOWFm
OC1jOTU5LTYwODEtMzliMS04ODg0YzgyYjYxYTAmaW5zaWQ9NTYxMg&ptn=3&hsh=
3&fclid=2aee9af8-c959-6081-39b1-
8884c82b61a0&u=a1L3NlYXJjaD9xPWRlZmluZStkb2NpbGUmRk9STT1EQlRSSUVVk&ntb
=1

17. https://www.bing.com/ck/
a?!&&p=0e0651240af87db3JmltdHM9MTY4MDA0ODAwMCZpZ3VpZD0yYWVlOWFm
OC1jOTU5LTYwODEtMzliMS04ODg0YzgyYjYxYTAmaW5zaWQ9NTYxMw&ptn=3&hsh=
3&fclid=2aee9af8-c959-6081-39b1-
8884c82b61a0&u=a1L3NlYXJjaD9xPWRlZmluZStzdWJtaXNzaXZlJkZPUk09RENUUlFZ&
ntb=1

18. https://www.bing.com/ck/
a?!&&p=6e57bfa44c28759eJmltdHM9MTY4MDA0ODAwMCZpZ3VpZD0yYWVlOWFmO
C1jOTU5LTYwODEtMzliMS04ODg0YzgyYjYxYTAmaW5zaWQ9NTYxNA&ptn=3&hsh=3
&fclid=2aee9af8-c959-6081-39b1-
8884c82b61a0&u=a1L3NlYXJjaD9xPWRlZmluZStvYmVkaWVudCZGT1JNPURDVFJRWQ
&ntb=1

19. https://www.bing.com/ck/
a?!&&p=c682cc625eda5bf4JmltdHM9MTY4MDA0ODAwMCZpZ3VpZD0yYWVlOWFmO
C1jOTU5LTYwODEtMzliMS04ODg0YzgyYjYxYTAmaW5zaWQ9NTYxNQ&ptn=3&hsh=3
&fclid=2aee9af8-c959-6081-39b1-
8884c82b61a0&u=a1L3NlYXJjaD9xPWRlZmluZSt0YW1lJkZPUk09RENUUlFZ&ntb=1

20. https://www.bing.com/ck/
a?!&&p=febf64dadbdf3051JmltdHM9MTY4MDA0ODAwMCZpZ3VpZD0yYWVlOWFmO

antonyms:

<u>uncooperative</u>[22]

- *(amenable to)*

capable of being acted upon in a particular way; susceptible:

"cardiac failure not amenable to medical treatment"

synonyms

susceptible[23] · receptive[24] · responsive[25] · reactive[26] · vulnerable[27] · defenceless against · susceptive[28]

C1jOTU5LTYwODEtMzliMS04ODg0YzgyYjYxYTAmaW5zaWQ9NTYxNg&ptn=3&hsh=3& fclid=2aee9af8-c959-6081-39b1-

8884c82b61a0&u=a1L3NlYXJjaD9xPWRlZmluZSttZWVVrJkZPUk09RENUUlFZ&ntb=1

21. https://www.bing.com/ck/

a?!&&p=63883b8a1e1dd9a4JmltdHM9MTY4MDA0ODAwMCZpZ3VpZD0yYWVlOWFm OC1jOTU5LTYwODEtMzliMS04ODg0YzgyYjYxYTAmaW5zaWQ9NTYxNw&ptn=3&hsh= 3&fclid=2aee9af8-c959-6081-39b1-

8884c82b61a0&u=a1L3NlYXJjaD9xPWRlZmluZStwZXJjdWFzaWJsZSZGT1JNPURDVFJR WQ&ntb=1

22. https://www.bing.com/ck/

a?!&&p=5d9527be22ff0b5cJmltdHM9MTY4MDA0ODAwMCZpZ3VpZD0yYWVlOWFmO C1jOTU5LTYwODEtMzliMS04ODg0YzgyYjYxYTAmaW5zaWQ9NTYxOQ&ptn=3&hsh=3 &fclid=2aee9af8-c959-6081-39b1-

8884c82b61a0&u=a1L3NlYXJjaD9xPWRlZmluZSt1bmNvb3BlcmF0aZlJkZPUk09RENUUl FZ&ntb=1

23. https://www.bing.com/ck/

a?!&&p=1068c2c9350e03bfJmltdHM9MTY4MDA0ODAwMCZpZ3VpZD0yYWVlOWFm OC1jOTU5LTYwODEtMzliMS04ODg0YzgyYjYxYTAmaW5zaWQ9NTYyMg&ptn=3&hsh=3 &fclid=2aee9af8-c959-6081-39b1-

8884c82b61a0&u=a1L3NlYXJjaD9xPWRlZmluZStzdXNjZXB0aWxpdZSZGT1JNPURDVFJR
WQ&ntb=1

24. https://www.bing.com/ck/
a?!&&p=80429482cac1a413JmltdHM9MTY4MDA0ODAwMCZpZ3VpZD0yYWVlOWFm
OC1jOTU5LTYwODEtMzliMS04ODg0Yzgy YjYxYTAmaW5zaWQ9NTYyMw&ptn=3&hsh=
3&fclid=2aee9af8-c959-6081-39b1-
8884c82b61a0&u=a1L3NlYXJjaD9xPWRlZmluZStyZWNlcHRpdmUmRk9STT1EQ1RSUV
k&ntb=1

25. https://www.bing.com/ck/
a?!&&p=7d62911b931968c9JmltdHM9MTY4MDA0ODAwMCZpZ3VpZD0yYWVlOWFm
OC1jOTU5LTYwODEtMzliMS04ODg0Yzgy YjYxYTAmaW5zaWQ9NTYyNA&ptn=3&hsh=
3&fclid=2aee9af8-c959-6081-39b1-
8884c82b61a0&u=a1L3NlYXJjaD9xPWRlZmluZStyZXNwb25zaXZlJkZPUk09RENUUlFZ
&ntb=1

26. https://www.bing.com/ck/
a?!&&p=944e9514d22cb6a2JmltdHM9MTY4MDA0ODAwMCZpZ3VpZD0yYWVlOWFm
OC1jOTU5LTYwODEtMzliMS04ODg0Yzgy YjYxYTAmaW5zaWQ9NTYyNQ&ptn=3&hsh=
3&fclid=2aee9af8-c959-6081-39b1-
8884c82b61a0&u=a1L3NlYXJjaD9xPWRlZmluZStyZWFjdGl2ZSZGT1JNPURDVFJRWQ&
ntb=1

27. https://www.bing.com/ck/
a?!&&p=b1cea304eaa24803JmltdHM9MTY4MDA0ODAwMCZpZ3VpZD0yYWVlOWFmO
C1jOTU5LTYwODEtMzliMS04ODg0Yzgy YjYxYTAmaW5zaWQ9NTYyNg&ptn=3&hsh=3&
fclid=2aee9af8-c959-6081-39b1-
8884c82b61a0&u=a1L3NlYXJjaD9xPWRlZmluZSt2dWxuZXJhYmxlJkZPUk09RENUUlFZ&
ntb=1

28. https://www.bing.com/ck/
a?!&&p=188ad3d350d83e0fJmltdHM9MTY4MDA0ODAwMCZpZ3VpZD0yYWVlOWFm
OC1jOTU5LTYwODEtMzliMS04ODg0Yzgy YjYxYTAmaW5zaWQ9NTYyNw&ptn=3&hsh=
3&fclid=2aee9af8-c959-6081-39b1-
8884c82b61a0&u=a1L3NlYXJjaD9xPWRlZmluZStzdXNjZXB0aWJsZSZGT1JNPURDVFJRWQ&
ntb=1

antonyms:

resistant[29]

ORIGIN

late 16th century (in the sense 'liable to answer to a law or tribunal'): an Anglo-Norman French legal term, from Old French amener 'bring to' from a- (from Latin ad) 'to' + mener 'bring' (from late Latin minare 'drive animals', from Latin minari 'threaten').

Choose language

Submissive, willing, or cooperative

Amenable synonym is a word that means **submissive, willing, or cooperative**[130][231][332][433]. Some examples of amenable synonyms are

29. https://www.bing.com/ck/
a?!&&p=0fe2df87623a4f8bJmltdHM9MTY4MDA0ODAwMCZpZ3VpZD0yYWVlOWFmO
C1jOTU5LTYwODEtMzliMS04ODg0YzgyYjYxYTAmaW5zaWQ9NTYyOQ&ptn=3&hsh=3
&fclid=2aee9af8-c959-6081-39b1-
8884c82b61a0&u=a1L3NlYXJjaD9xPWRlZmluZStyZXNpc3RhbnQmRk9STT1EQlRSSUVVk
&ntb=1

30. https://www.bing.com/ck/
a?!&&p=c7358af11dbc0805JmltdHM9MTY4MDA0ODAwMCZpZ3VpZD0yYWVlOWFmOC1jOTU5LTYwODEtMzli
MS04ODg0YzgyYjYxYTAmaW5zaWQ9NTQwOQ&ptn=3&hsh=3&fclid=2aee9af8-c959-6081-39b1-
8884c82b61a0&psq=amenable+synonym&u=a1aHR0cHM6Ly93d3cuc3lub255bXMuY29tL3N5bm9ueW0vYW1lbmFibG
U&ntb=1

31. https://www.bing.com/ck/
a?!&&p=ee5c525d6cc7ac60JmltdHM9MTY4MDA0ODAwMCZpZ3VpZD0yYWVlOWFmOC1jOTU5LTYwODEtMzli
MS04ODg0YzgyYjYxYTAmaW5zaWQ9NTQxMA&ptn=3&hsh=3&fclid=2aee9af8-c959-6081-39b1-
8884c82b61a0&psq=amenable+synonym&u=a1aHR0cHM6Ly90aGVzYXVydXMucGx1cy9zeW5vbnltcy9hbWVuYWJsZQ
&ntb=1

32. https://www.bing.com/ck/
a?!&&p=f15037d06bd81a69JmltdHM9MTY4MDA0ODAwMCZpZ3VpZD0yYWVlOWFmOC1jOTU5LTYwODEtMzli
MS04ODg0YzgyYjYxYTAmaW5zaWQ9NTQxMQ&ptn=3&hsh=3&fclid=2aee9af8-c959-6081-39b1-

liable, agreeable, receptive, compliant, ready, accommodating, tractable, docile, obedient, responsive, and susceptible[31,32,33,34,35,36,37,38]. Amenable also means able to be judged or responsible[39,40]. Some

8884c82b61a0&psq=amenable+synonym&u=a1aHR0cHM6Ly93d3cubWVycmlhbbS13ZWJzdGVyLmNvbS90aGVzYXVyXMvYW1lbmFibGU&ntb=1

33. https://www.bing.com/ck/
a?!&&p=e973ab1119c39f5fJmltdHM9MTY4MDA0ODAwMCZpZ3VpZD0yYWVlOWFmOC1jOTU5LTYwODEtMzli
MS04ODg0YzgyYjYxYTAmaW5zaWQ9NTQxMg&ptn=3&hsh=3&fclid=2aee9af8-c959-6081-39b1-
8884c82b61a0&psq=amenable+synonym&u=a1aHR0cHM6Ly93d3cudGhlc2F1cnVzLmNvbS9icm93c2UvYW1lbmFibG
U&ntb=1

34. https://www.bing.com/ck/
a?!&&p=98e917bb3041efbbJmltdHM9MTY4MDA0ODAwMCZpZ3VpZD0yYWVlOWFmOC1jOTU5LTYwODEtMzli
MS04ODg0YzgyYjYxYTAmaW5zaWQ9NTQxMw&ptn=3&hsh=3&fclid=2aee9af8-c959-6081-39b1-
8884c82b61a0&psq=amenable+synonym&u=a1aHR0cHM6Ly93d3cuc3lub255bXMuY29tL3N5bm9ueW0vYW1lbmFibG
U&ntb=1

35. https://www.bing.com/ck/
a?!&&p=939397eb0013ee3dJmltdHM9MTY4MDA0ODAwMCZpZ3VpZD0yYWVlOWFmOC1jOTU5LTYwODEtMzli
MS04ODg0YzgyYjYxYTAmaW5zaWQ9NTQxNA&ptn=3&hsh=3&fclid=2aee9af8-c959-6081-39b1-
8884c82b61a0&psq=amenable+synonym&u=a1aHR0cHM6Ly90aGVzYXVydXMucGx1cy9zeW5vbnltcy9hbWVuYWJsZQ
&ntb=1

36. https://www.bing.com/ck/
a?!&&p=7ca1bcb3d0d2beadJmltdHM9MTY4MDA0ODAwMCZpZ3VpZD0yYWVlOWFmOC1jOTU5LTYwODEtMzli
MS04ODg0YzgyYjYxYTAmaW5zaWQ9NTQxNQ&ptn=3&hsh=3&fclid=2aee9af8-c959-6081-39b1-
8884c82b61a0&psq=amenable+synonym&u=a1aHR0cHM6Ly93d3cubWVycmlhbbS13ZWJzdGVyLmNvbS90aGVzYXVyXMvYW1lbmFibGU&ntb=1

37. https://www.bing.com/ck/
a?!&&p=f9bd9f545a61e13cJmltdHM9MTY4MDA0ODAwMCZpZ3VpZD0yYWVlOWFmOC1jOTU5LTYwODEtMzliM
S04ODg0YzgyYjYxYTAmaW5zaWQ9NTQxNg&ptn=3&hsh=3&fclid=2aee9af8-c959-6081-39b1-
8884c82b61a0&psq=amenable+synonym&u=a1aHR0cHM6Ly93d3cudGhlc2F1cnVzLmNvbS9icm93c2UvYW1lbmFibG
U&ntb=1

38. https://www.bing.com/ck/
a?!&&p=75ee99a7e6e9d18fJmltdHM9MTY4MDA0ODAwMCZpZ3VpZD0yYWVlOWFmOC1jOTU5LTYwODEtMzli
MS04ODg0YzgyYjYxYTAmaW5zaWQ9NTQxNw&ptn=3&hsh=3&fclid=2aee9af8-c959-6081-39b1-
8884c82b61a0&psq=amenable+synonym&u=a1aHR0cHM6Ly90aGVzYXVydXMueW91cmRpY3Rpb25hcnkuY29tL2FtZ
W5hYmxl&ntb=1

39. https://www.bing.com/ck/
a?!&&p=506773ae030756e8JmltdHM9MTY4MDA0ODAwMCZpZ3VpZD0yYWVlOWFmOC1jOTU5LTYwODEtMzli
MS04ODg0YzgyYjYxYTAmaW5zaWQ9NTQxOA&ptn=3&hsh=3&fclid=2aee9af8-c959-6081-39b1-
8884c82b61a0&psq=amenable+synonym&u=a1aHR0cHM6Ly93d3cudGhlc2F1cnVzLmNvbS9icm93c2UvYW1lbmFibG
U&ntb=1

40. https://www.bing.com/ck/
a?!&&p=526727174bf1b48dJmltdHM9MTY4MDA0ODAwMCZpZ3VpZD0yYWVlOWFmOC1jOTU5LTYwODEtMzli

antonyms of amenable are independent, autocratic, unamenable, irresponsible, refractory, and obstinate[141]

THE FUNERAL IS NOT a problem. Maureen simply reacts to other people's distress, which is just another form of amenable after all. Tea and biscuits later are a little harder to manage. A smile insists on creeping into her mind, so she keeps her eyes lowered and specs only in monosyllables. No one notices.

They all think she is half-mad, or stupid, or both. Everyone's eyes are on Lebo, waiting for her to give way to a distasteful show of grief. After all, Lebo is Dave's mistress. Was Dave's lover. The day it happened began no differently than a hundred other Saturdays. Dave shaved, showered, wolfed down his food, then left for work without saying a word although he had muttered a disgusted "tsk tsk" when she walked out of the room wearing the pink silk negligee, a gift from Dave during their courting days, it was now worn and faded like her; but the newer purple chenille dressing gown needed to be washed.

Her breakfast was an apple and a cup of black coffee. Dave wanted her to lose at least four kilos. Two birds with one stone, cut down on the food bill and spare the expense of new clothes. The lingering waft of his bacon and eggs

tempted her, but the habit of amenable was too strong. Tying back her frizzy hair with a length of wool, she wandered into the bathroom to read the list of instructions he taped to the mirror each morning. This never failed to amuse her. She hadn't looked into a mirror for years.

1. Check to see if cows number 44 and 52 have calved.

MS04ODg0YzgyYjYxYTAmaW5zaWQ9NTQxOQ&ptn=3&hsh=3&fclid=2aee9af8-c959-6081-39b1-8884c82b61a0&psq=amenable+synonym&u=a1aHR0cHM6Ly90aGVzYXVydXMuW91cmRpY3Rpb25hcnkuY29tL2FtZW5hYmxl&ntb=1

41. https://www.bing.com/ck/
a?!&&p=0087e468415248eaJmltdHM9MTY4MDA0ODAwMCZpZ3VpZD0yYWVlOWFmOC1jOTU5LTYwODEtMzli
MS04ODg0YzgyYjYxYTAmaW5zaWQ9NTQyMA&ptn=3&hsh=3&fclid=2aee9af8-c959-6081-39b1-8884c82b61a0&psq=amenable+synonym&u=a1aHR0cHM6Ly93d3cuc3lub255bXMuY29tL3N5bm9ueW0vYW1lbmFibGF U&ntb=1

2. New bull pushed water trough off stand. Fix it, water and feed him!

3. Weed Garden.

4. Washing, don't forget your dressing gown again.

5. Ironing

6. Clean stove.

The instructions went up to 12. She didn't mind. Dave had always been a diligent worker, and he expected the same from her. Although while his poor city beginnings had given him a need for wealth and respect, she thought it was all a waste of time. Nothing held her interest any more.

Sometimes she thought about dying. The trouble was, she didn't believe in suicide, and she had been cursed with longevity genes. Her mother had died young, but only to spite her father. He died from a fall after swearing the ghost of his wife had pitchforked the horse. Yet all the other ancestors had easily passed 90. Dave didn't know about them. He'd clearly stated that he expected her to dutifully depart this world around the age 50. She smiled at the irony. She'd inherited her mother's spitefulness. She decided to do the gardening first.

Perhaps she'd cut roses for the convicts' graves near the creek, even though he laughed at her for continuing this custom which was started by her paternal grandmother. He laughed about Grandmother, too, forgetting that the old lady had doubled the size of this farm. Dave had sold most of those added acres to buy properties in Pretoria - all in Maureen's name so the farm could help reduce the taxes. After she died, in a year or two, five at the most. Dave would reap his rightful rewards. For now, she could just be sensible and sign the cheques. Or so he always said.

Her bank manager had hinted with meaningful looks and many hums and hahs that signing cheques without question could be considered rather stupid. But Dave had always been clever with business. The bank balance and property assets continued to grow under his management. Maureen had to agree with the banker. She was stupid, like her grandmother. She was drowning on her hands and knees, enjoying the smell of earth and freshly cut roses, when a blue sedan rattled through the gateway.

Standing slowly, she stared along the winding track leading up to the highway. Nobody came to see her anymore. The people in the car would be looking for Dave. He sold real estate on weekends. They would see she hadn't bothered to dress. That was another bad habit she'd picked up since her daughter Layla left - like preferring her own company to theirs and conversing with the dogs. Now there'd be new rumours about old Rummy Tom's eccentric daughter. Runs in the family, they'd say.

They'd feel sorry for Dave and buy more goods from his store instead of going to the competition. Whitewood's shop, the only other general store in Pretoria, was run by a straitlaced and godly pair. No gossip there. No chance to watch Lebo and Dave exchanging secret smiles.

She wanted to run and hide, but Dave's instructions had been perfectly clear. If anyone comes, send them straight to the store. "He's not here," she called. "His office is in

Pretoria. That's three kilometres down the highway. You can't miss it - there are no houses until you get there." A tall, thin man unwound from the car, managing not to look amused or shocked by this frowsy woman in soiled pink negligee.

"Maureen Simmons?" he asked hesitantly, seeming to doubt the question, then her nod of affirmation. Frowning, he glanced past her to the house before finally offering a thin white object "I live in the flat next to Layla. She asked me to give you this."

Maureen's hands closed to the fists. It was an involuntary reaction, but Dave had never actually forbidden her to accept mail. The mail carrier usually delivered it to the office. She snatched the envelope out of the tall man's hand.

"I told her last night that I was heading out this way. Holidays, you know?" he said. "She gave me the note this morning."

Maureen hugged the letter to her chest. She wanted to ask this man in for a cup of tea or a glass of lemonade. Maybe bacon and egg if the hens had laid. She could cut the strips of bacon into paper thin slices so Dave wouldn't realise that some was missing. Anything to keep this man here while she asked about the baby, about how Layla lived, who her friends were. If she'd let her hair grow long again. If she still had that cheeky grin. She thrust the roses into his hand.

The hint of derision faded from his eyes. He reached out with one finger and brushed a tear from her cheek.

No one had touched her since Layla left. She tried to thank him, but the words would not form. It was too long since she had talked with a stranger. Since she had talked at all. He smiled reassurance and turned away.

As Maureen watched his car disappear, she stroked the envelope lightly with the cushions of her fingertips while imagining the texture of Layla's skin. She touched the scrawled name and imagined touching Layla's cheek. She turned the envelope over, smiling at the strip of Sellotape sealing the flap like a band-aid covering a cut knee. careful not to hurt, she scratched up the edges of the tape and gently eased it away.

Inside was a single sheet of paper. Once pristine it was now soiled and crumpled by indifferent hands. Slowly, she filled the envelope with petals and lay it on the ground. Savouring was always better than having. It was a gas bill. Surely Layla knew that Dave never left money in the house. He managed all the expenses. Wait, the back was covered in Layla's untidy scrawl. Smoothing the street, Maureen read aloud............

"I am sorry, Mom. They took the baby last night. They said I was unfit. He won't let me come home and I've got nowhere else. Michael left a month ago and I don't know how to be alone. I have been saving sleeping pills; I know you can't help it. I can't help it either. Love you. Layla."

The scream followed her to the gate. It began again when there was no sign of the blue car, or any other. It continued tearing at her throat as she stumbled and ran three kilometres to the small town in Pretoria. There was a phone booth outside the caravan park, but she had no money and the operator asked questions she couldn't answer. Her voice lay somewhere on the road along with her screams.

She ran from the booth but forgot to release the receiver. It jerked her backwards in a stumbling fall. She hit the back of the booth, then fell forward in a tangle of arms and legs. Two boys riding tandem on a 10-speed bike stopped to stare down at the mad woman with a negligee around her neck. She tried to show them the letter. One snatched it out of her hand and pedalled away.

The other one ran beside him. Their laughter thudded between her eyes like a closed fist. She caught up with them at the next corner and threw the rider off the bike and onto his friend with one backhanded sweep of her arm.

Snatching the letter, she pedalled into the main street, still trying to scream Layla's name. The boys ignored their coating of pebbles and raced after her. Their yells mingled with her shrieks brought Dave racing out of the store. Maureen remembers the look on Dave's face. The mourners are shocked by her sudden snort of laughter. She turns it into a cough. The minister hurries forward to pat her back. She sprays him with orange cream biscuit. Maureen's second snort of laughter is hidden by the crush of Pretoria ladies rushing to brush him down. The minister is an unmarried person and competition are fierce. She adds to the confusion with a surreptitious tweak of his thigh before wandering outside for the more appealing company of her dogs.

She watches as they greet a visiting car. Lebo follows her into the veranda but turns her back on the dogs. Their method of introduction and identification offends her city bred sensibilities. "The roses are beautiful," she says in her carefully modulated, well-educated voice. "Mom planted them before she died," Maureen says dreamily. "Dad wanted to rip them out, but he couldn't be bothered. Layla loved them, too."

Lebo's sigh is as carefully modulated as her voice and clothes. "It must have been hard for you," she murmurs. "I believe your father was a very difficult man with rather strange habits. Or so the people in Pretoria say."

Maureen shrugs. "He just liked to dress in Mom's clothes. And he was all right with me as long as I did what I was told." She gave Lebo a sideways glance. "It gets to be a habit. Like it did with Dave."

Lebo's voice is a little rough around the edges as she replies, "You chose to marry him."

"I thought he'd take me away from here," Maureen sighs. "But then dad died, and Dave said if we waited the farm would be worth more. We waited too long past the boom. Do not think he wanted to go really."

"You shouldn't blame him for making Layla leave," Lebo whispers. "He could not abide the shame of a wayward daughter. He was hard, but you must admire him. What is a man without principles?" Maureen does not remind Lebo of the proviso in dad's will. Equal share of the farm between Maureen and Layla, if Maureen never signed any of it over to her husband and Layla stayed until she was of legal age. Dave turned her out of the house a month before her 18th birthday. Although, to be fair to Dave, Layla had wanted to go. She stopped calling him 'dad' a month after Lebo came to Pretoria.

Thinking of Pretoria reminds Maureen of Dave's face again. Pretoria turned out to stare at the mute mad woman cycling along the main street in a tattered pink silk negligee.

Maureen bent low over the handlebars, pedalling hard to stay in front of the boys. While they ran, they leapt into the air trying to grab her negligee as it flared out in her slipstream. One finally managed to grab a ruff of pink lace, which was enough to make her lose control. The bike threw her onto the footpath in front of Dave. She tried to force out the words to tell him about Layla, but they were caught somewhere down in her throat.

She wheezed and gasped, raking at her tongue and cheeks and tearing at her hair. When a crowd gathered, Dave mumbled something about that certain time of life and bundled her into the store. Lebo prised the letter out of her fingers and she gave her water to wet her throat so Maureen could speak.

She also gave her a handful of tranquillisers and did not notice when she spat them out. Back at the funeral, Maureen remembers how Lebo's need to be seen as a compassionate person had saved Layla's life. She wonders if the deed is more important than the reason. She shrugs away the thought as being too complicated for her simple mind and turns to watch a taxi move slowly down the track from the highway. This time she does not try to hide the brightness of her eyes.

Lebo is clutching her arm. The urgency is transferred. Maureen faces her. "I just want you to know that I never meant you any harm," Lebo says. "I knew him a long time ago. We were childhood sweethearts. Meeting him again......" She stops to sighs. "I never meant you any harm." Maureen pats Lebo's shoulder. What else can she do? After the farm accident, the police had questioned Lebo first. She had confessed to giving Maureen the tranquillisers and they knew Dave's lover wouldn't lie about that. Lebo had confirmed the town's opinion that Maureen is more simple than insane, and the police agreed that stupidity is akin to innocence. And Lebo had saved Layla's life.

Dave had refused to speak to her as he drove Maureen back to the farm that day. He was angry at her for casting a slur on his reputation. as owner of the general store and a council member, he had an image to uphold.

Hale buff Dave may not be so hearty after all. Why didn't his wife have a car, the Pretorians were asking each other. Why could not she use the homestead phone. He reminded them of her father, Rummy Tom, the funny dresser. And of Tom's older sister, weird Margaret the greenie. Turned eighty now and still running around the country hugging trees. And what about Grandma gathering roses for century-dead convicts, and Maureen hardly ever coming into Pretoria anymore? He wiped a drool of water from her chin and called attention to the faded pink negligee. What normal woman wears such a thing to town?

Maureen merely looked up at him and smiled. The ambulance had reached Layla in time. Back at the farm, she refused to finish the chores and staggered off to bed, pretending to be under the influence of tranquillisers. A small triumph, but a heady one. Perhaps she would baulk at making dinner. It was time to make a stand. Layla had always said that people used her. Dave said she liked to be used, and some people were born wimps. Maureen's mother had once said that she'd been born with a habit of obedience.

He stood over the bed and glared. Her resolve disappeared. She tried to say she would start with the cows. "Not one word" he said sternly. "I do not want to hear your voice. I will do the chores you neglected. Meanwhile I have unlocked the phone, but you are not to use it, nor are you to leave this room until I give my permission."

She watched through the window as he checked numbers 44 and 52. They had not calved. Next on his list was the bull. That's when she remembered that it hadn't been fed and watered. She leaned through the window to call out a warning. But Dave had said he did not want to hear her voice. The bull charged out of the shed as Dave walked through the gate way. He jumped back but didn't have time to throw the bolt.

The animal slammed into the gate, which slammed into Dave, hurling him flat out on his back in the middle of the track. Maureen could have called out and told him that the bull just wanted to reach the water trough. All he had to do was lie still. But he had forbidden her to speak. Dave staggered to his feet and tried to run. He was between that bull and the trough. He never had a chance.

Maureen watched the animal drink his fill, then wander away to eat.

She could have left the room and telephone for help. But the habit of obedience was too strong. "If only I hadn't given you those tranquillisers," Lebo says at the funeral. "If he hadn't lain there all day, he'd still be alive now. If only I'd come before dark to see why he wasn't answering the phone."

"So many ifs," Maureen agrees sadly. "It could be the wrong time to raise this issue," Lebo says, "but I've worked for next to nothing and invested all my savings in the properties Dave acquired. Of course, we never signed a contract, but Dave told me that he'd changed his will, leaving the townhouse and half the store to me. You can't run the shop, and I don't want to leave. I'll sell the house and buy out your share. I will even take some of those other places off your hands if you like. They'd just keep you away from the farm."

The taxi stops, Layla and her baby are inside, Maureen is packed and ready to go. A new life with her daughter and granddaughter. They'd go far from the farm perhaps to the city and live among strangers. It would be difficult at first, but with Layla's help she'd be able to break all the old habits. Lebo holds her arm waiting for an answer. Maureen knows that Dave had never made a will. He had nothing to leave. Everything is in Maureen's name. Of course, she could mention these facts, but she'd never been good at words but observe. And Lebo had saved Layla's life. The least Maureen owes her is a few days of dreaming. The lawyers will give Dave's mistress the true facts when she tries to make a claim. And Lebo's voice had a tone of authority, so of course Maureen agrees to everything that she says.

Time passed by, firstly was days, weeks then months, and now Lebo thought she had all under control and the future looked brighter than she excepted. The farm, the property and the store will be under her control, and she could do anything she ever thought of now without limitation.

Maureen was not too sure if she neither approach her nor leave her to be daydreaming.

Though time was not on their sides both. Within a year letter from the Lawyers arrived at Lebo's house with full documentation of the rightful beneficiaries. Now embarrassment was full on her face she had nowhere to hide but face the reality. But as Maureen was well raised and was humble, she offered her a job at the shop to keep the legacy of her father going.

With the mourning long face on Maureen's face, I saw a lost soul and an opportunity at the same time. Maureen and I had been neighbours for years in Pretoria, even though it was quiet a distance. We were good friends. Our better halves had both been no more, which had made for an amicable rivalry, when we still could, before their departure.

When Maureen and I were widowed within a year of each other, our friendship helped us both get through the pain. We continued seeing each other and on alternate Wednesday we played scrabble, which I often won, or cards. Maureen never failed to beat me at whist. It was while we were playing scrabble one evening that Maureen suddenly sighed. I thought it was because I was beating her again, but no........ "I wish I could get away for a few days, out of Pretoria maybe," she said.

"It's been 13 months since Dave died, I have not had a break in all time."

"Do you have somewhere specific in mind?" "Absolutely anywhere," she replied me.

I laughed. "You should go."

"I am not sure I can. Nothing by myself." She sighed again and added an S to a six-letter word, giving her the best score of the evening.

"Oh, I know I'm being silly and lots of people go away on their own, but....."

That is when I had the idea.

"Well, we could always go together," I suggested. "Really?" she looked so surprised I laughed again. "Why not?"

"Obviously we'd have separate rooms."

21

For a split second I thought she looked disappointed, but I decided it was probably my imagination. I mean, we were friends, but there had never been the faintest spark between us, as Dave was a friend too. We were just too different for anything like that. "So where shall we go, then?" I said. "I was thinking Thailand. Maybe Chiang Mai."

"Gracious me, No," I said. "I haven't been overseas since I was at school."

My late wife always said South Africa was more than enough for her, and I agreed.

"Okay, then. How about Cape Town? Fish and chips, great beaches, surfing."

I had been there with Wendy a few times. She'd loved to go up there to an excellent local theatre they had near Muizenburg. We'd catch the train up, go to a matinée and travel home again on the same day. Apart from that, I had no experience of the area. That all seemed a little too cheap and cheerful for my late wife's liking.

I was about to suggest somewhere else when I noticed the expression on Maureen's face. She looked so excited and happy, like a Labrador being shown a lead. "Okay, then, Cape Town it is," I said.

I was put in charge of travel arrangements. I didn't think Maureen would be comfortable in an expensive hotel, as I thought she had lost everything to Lebo after Dave died, so I chose a mid-range one, in Gordon's Bay, close to the beach.

I booked five nights long enough to feel like you'd been away, but not too long in case we got on each other's nerves. As to what we would do when we got there, I suggested she decides that day and I the next. That way we'd both get to do things we enjoyed at least some of the times.

On our first day, it was my choice. I'd browsed the internet for museums and gallery and Cape Gardens. It sat on the water and had a great cafe, as well as the gallery and a beautiful formal garden out the back.

While I read the brochures about upcoming activities, Maureen wandered the gallery, oohing and ahhing over various sculptures and paintings. We wandered out into the gardens dappled with cherry blossoms and ornamental sculptures. Every now and then she asked me to take her photo, which was distracting, especially when I was trying to take in some facts and figures about local culture. But at least she was having fun.

After lunch in the hotel, we went to a nearby museum, which was all about local geology. I confess that even I found that a bit dry. We did not stay very long as Maureen was starting to get a bit fidgety. As the sun was shining, I suggested a stroll along the waterfront. It wasn't long before Maureen spotted her favourite ice-cream parlour.

"What flavour do you fancy?"

"Not for me, thanks. I am not very keen on ice-cream." She looked at me as though I was insane. "But we're at the beach,"

The shop had a vast display of flavours. The choice was mind boggling. Everything from bubble gum- a ghastly shade of electric blue to lemon sherbet. Maureen grinned. "I think I have spotted one that you'll like. Let me get it for you," she insisted. "My treaty."

"If you must, but I don't promise to eat it."

"Not a problem." She grinned. "I can finish two."

She made me close my eyes, then whispered her order to the salesperson. When I opened my eyes again, she handed me a small tub of ice-cream so dark it was almost black.

Reluctantly, I put a tiny amount on the spoon and licked it. To my surprise, the taste was amazing. I rarely ate desserts or sweets, but liquorice, well, that was something else entirely. I wondered if Maureen knew that somehow, or whether it was just a lucky guess.

As I began to tuck into the ice-cream, Maureen clapped her hands.

"See? I knew you'd like it."

That evening we ate at the hotel. The dining room was elegant and full of light, but there was not much of view. When I said as much to

Maureen, she smiled. "The best views aren't confined to the best hotels." That was a reference to the kind of hotel she might have stayed at with Dave, but I was mistaken. According to Maureen, the best view was on Dave's farm looking down on a long road down to his shop in Pretoria. Except the beach, eating lunch out of a box.

We began the next day with a tour of the traveling fair. I was not keen. Too much noise and too many bright lights. But Maureen had a great time, pushing coins into slots and making bets on plastic clowns. After that we played a few rounds of ten pin bowling, followed by a go on the dodgem cars. I could not believe how competitive Maureen was. Because I won most of the bowling games, She threw herself into the dodgems and I was battered to pulp in no time at all. "Hold on, give me a chance!" I shouted, gripping the wheel of my little car.

"No way," she said, laughing. Then she rammed the front of her car into mine. "Take that!"

It was a lot more fun than I'd expected, but I didn't tell Maureen that. We had fish and chips for lunch. If it had been up to me, we would have gone to a restaurant instead, we sat on the sea wall, watching people taking a dip in the ocean. Maureen seemed so contented, kicking her legs back and forth, like a child at the beach for the first time.

"What have you got planned for this afternoon?" I asked, hardly daring to think what she might have in store.

I imagined we would be paddling or splashing through rock pools searching for crabs. "Well, you'll have to wait and see," she said. Whatever it was it had to be better than another noisy round at the fair.

"Don't worry," she said. "You will love it."

She was right. Again.

We went to a local vintage museum. It was wonderland and full of someof the things I loved most in the world, like vintage cars and motorbikes along with several beautifully restored fairground organs. They were all in working order, too.

The entrance fee included a free go on one of the rides. Maureen could hardly wait. She headed straight for the carousel and climbed onto one of the grinning horses. "Come join me," she said. "It's great fun."

To say I was not very keen went nowhere near the truth.

"No thanks, Maureen. I would rather watch."

As the music started, the garishly painted horses came to life. And when they began to pick up speed, Maureen called out to me.

"Don't just stand there! Take my photo." Each time Maureen's horse came around, she waved and posed for a picture. "That was amazing!" she said, when the carousel finally stopped. She jumped down from the horse and wobbled as her feet hit the ground. I dashed to hold her elbow to steady her.

"Thanks," she said, her eyes bright. "I'd have another go, but it doesn't run again for an hour." There was so much to see that we were still there an hour later. Maureen kept looking over at the carousel. I handed her my ticket. "Have one on me," I said.

It was a lovely afternoon. When we left, I could still hear the glorious sounds of those fairground organs. We caught a bus back to Gordon's Bay then strolled to the hotel for our dinner. By the time we'd finished eating it was late. All I wanted was

my bed. It had been a long day.

When I woke up the next morning, my head felt as though it was full of candy floss. I didn't fancy breakfast, especially when a glance out of the window at a crisp blue sky. What I wanted was a walk. On my way downstairs, I knocked on Maureen's bedroom door. When she opened it, she was in her dressing gown, her hair slightly tousled. I had not realised how early it was. "Sorry to disturb you," I said. "Only I'm skipping breakfast this morning in favour of a brisk walk." she seemed disappointed, but then she put on a smile.

"Have an enjoyable time. I will catch up with you later." As I set off, I thought about my late wife and how very different she and Maureen were. Wend y had been quite intense and very serious about all kinds of things, especially her work. I couldn't picture her whizzing about on dodgem cars or riding on a carousel.

Apart from few dog walkers, I had the beach to myself. Every breath I took seemed so pure it was like taking in gallon of sunshine. It felt good to be alive. After a while, I sat on the wall to browse the photos I had taken on my phone the day before. Among the traction engines and organs were pictures of Maureen on the carousel. I could not look at them without smiling. Her joy was so infectious, it made me think of other happy times in my life. Once I'd rested, I walked to the edge of the shore where a lump of driftwood had been thrown up onto the beach. I dragged it behind me, leaving a deep groove in the sand. It gave me an idea. I could use the piece of driftwood to write a letter in the sand. I was looking for shells to outline it when I hear Maureen's voice. "I love you too," she said.

She pointed at the letter in the sand. I was about to say it was W for Wendy, not M....... but when I saw the love in Maureen's eyes it was as if the blinds had been lifted. I'd loved my wife and always would. But in that moment, I knew I loved Maureen, too, and wanted her to be part of my life. I took her in my arms. "So, what shall we do today?" "Its your turn, today" she said.

I whispered in her ear. "How about returning to where we went yesterday? Then we could both have a ride on the carousel."

SIX MONTHS LATER, WHEN we were on our honeymoon, Maureen finally admitted the truth. She knew all along that it was a W I'd written in the sand that day, but, like she said, if she'd waited for me to make a move....... could have never happened.

At first, she has forgotten all her hometown Pretoria, however there is no place like home. The farm and shop, and her flowers had no one to care for this time, only the bulls, as she had decided to get someone to assist her after the passing of Dave.

However now the memories of her late husband still lingering at the back of her head, with his farmer's voice:

1. Check to see if cows' number 44 and 52 have calved.

2. New bull pushed water trough off stand. Fix it, water, and feed him.

3. Weed Garden.

4. Washing, do not forget your dressing gown again.

5. Ironing

6. Clean stove.

Though now it was written in her memory, and she was willing to be amenable and live serving Dave with honour.

"To the living we owe respect, but to the dead we only owe the Truth!" Voltaire.

END

THE SITUATIONSHIP!!

LITTLE BIRDS CHIPPING, they are singing a song, not because they have anything to say but because they are happier. We all are full of curiosity, for a reason or for no reason but that makes us humans because we always wonder why, what, who, when or how.

A little sleepy on the mall's little resting bench, at the back of my mind I see this short but not too short, blue short pants, this now mesmerize my mind. I might be dreaming, but no! Is this some kind of vision! Damn if it is a dream, please do not wake me up! You know God gave us all his best but trust me that was like something I never seen before.

The imaginary world of mine became reality as she opened her babbling lips... "Hi, do you mind if we share the bench sir?" with a soft gentle voice. I looked at her but I couldn't speak. I think she might have thought I was deaf or something. God have mess on us men, when she was closer I could see her small blue eyes a little short nose, now my heart was pounding like I've been chased by dogs', so I moved a little allowing her to have a seat closer to me. Now this is only when I realized I was not dreaming she was really beautiful.

I was nervous like never before; I did not know how I could start a conversation with her all I did was stare at her without blinking to a point she realized it and said, "Are you going to say something or just stare at me like you saw a ghost?" "Ummmmmm sorry ma'am", I replied with a little cough as there was something on my throat . "I think I've seen you before ma'am, ... maybe I am just mistaken?" I now replied with my calm deep voice like a SOTHO Warrior. She stare at me then she responds 'You're a funny guy.... why you calling me Ma'am like 1 1 m some kind of old lady? With a giggle I then knew this was my only chance to show her what I was made of.

Nowadays it's hard to find a single beautiful girl who has no husband or boyfriend. But I had to take a chance. 1 SO you live around this area1 without delay I asked with curiosity. And she nodded 1Yes I do and you are? Now she smiled with her beautiful white teeth. 1 1 1 m Joel but people call me Jo, what's your name girl', now I had confident as she was engaging with me. "Nicole! I am just gonna use the toilet 1 /1 1 be back now!" A loud voice from behind and I turned around there was this giant lady. "Now you know my name, and that's my aunt". She replied. I had no idea what was going on in her mind but to hell with that I am more focused on her. I had to get her numbers but only to find out she doesn't have a cellphone and that was now painful to me as I didn't know if she was telling the truth or lies. But I didnt let that stop me I had to continue. "Nicole, I am quiet lost, can you please direct me?" With a smile I asked. 'Where is it that you want to go?" curiously she replied. Without wasting no time I responded with my eyes staring her dead in the eye,"To your heart!".

She smiled continuously, 'Nice one" now she laughed, but I didn't blink until she was shy then with a soft voice"Well it's not easy to get to my heart,as there is already someone!' 1"But I will give you this, you got damn nerve!" she finalize.l couldn't just let go from start as everyone has someone but if it's yours put a ring on it. So when I looked down to her fingers I did see no ring. Now I couldn't just let her go just like that. "You atleast let me take you for a tea or coffee to apologize, for my heart, but 1 1 m not gonna take a no for an answer" now with confidence I asked her,though I could see in her eyes she was into me but because of her aunt who was with her she couldn't show off. "OKAY THEN I TELL YOU WHAT,let me think about it till tomorrow give me your number 1 /1 1 call you" she finally responded with what I needed to hear.

Time passed by, days passed by and a week passed by, and no word from her neither a call nor a message, did she lied to me. Definitely she did, but I got her word she will contact me. Sun set brilliantly on a Thursday evening, though there were signs of storm. In few hours the storm arrived, but it wasn't severe as hard storm. I was now preparing to go sleep as when storm breaks most bachelors feel lonely. Playing my favorite songs from PASSENGER not loudly but mid, I heard a knock on my door. Who could be this, and its raining and it's at night. I didn't really concern myself as I thought it was my neighbor's friends as they usually come visit her.

Another knock again and again and its getting harder then I got irritated and went to pull my Sig Sauer P239 pistol from my safe. Immediately safety off, slowly walking to the door as I knew I dont have visitors. I slowly opened the door "Jesus Christ, why you take long to open the door,look now I am wet, f##k!you got a gun at me" an aggresive woman voice with a little anger on it. I couldn't believe my eyes,mi mind was running through all the memories of people but no it was blank, this was really Nicole. I let her in however before I closed my door I checked if there was anyone following her but i couldn't see further as it was dark. "What are you doing here, Nicole!?" I was now confused on how she got my address, why did she come to my place in the first place."You know if I caught you unexpectedly I can leave!" she grabbed her bag walking towards the door.

I wanted her to leave and stay at the same time, now I walk towards the safe putting my little toy in the safe, I replied softly with a concerned voice "How did you get my address, How did you know where I live, is there anything I can help with." She smiled,"You really have no manners, do you" she responded shaking her head to rinse her wet hair. She was really wet the rain got her well and after a while I realized my floor was now full of water."Oh no, you're cold. I dont have women clothes but I think this will help,the toilet is on your left hand side". I gave her my night gown my favorite one my only gown and now I was left wearing only boxers short,she rushed to the toilet and I heard water running in the shower I knew it was her. But I didn't believe it still she was in my house.l opened my fridge to see what I could offer her to eat but I realized tea was the only solution to her coldness. I made tea for both of us and played cards.

We enjoyed our time until I fell asleep as we were watching TV. She left that night without saying anything and I couldn't kiss her no say bye that night. I woke up in the morning thinking maybe I was just too lonely and start seeing things that are not there. I went to take a shower but I noticed something different. Wait! Did she! Oh no was my mother here?. The whole room was extra clean everything on place like never before. She had cleaned my whole room to an extent that even my cat was washed.l now trying to find something left by her,oh no! She didn't left anything at all. As I was about to open the door,there she was coming by the door about to knock. "Who cleaned here, Where are my stuff,Why did you do that!" I shouted at her now. But she calmly said"l couldn't just leave my friend's house dirt after I messed it with water last night". "Friends!?" "Now we friends."

I was angry at her as to why she was being nice to me,but could say no dnt do it too cause I really liked her. She understood me my moods, my craziness to a point I was confused to how. Now I asked her to come by later after work for a movie and she didn't have a problem.

My day was greatest as I couldn't wait to get home for a movie night. As soon I got home I started spraying some perfume all around the house to impress her. She finally came with both popcorns. As I didnt have chairs nor couches i asked her to seat on my bed and she jumped with her shoes on and i did not like it but i couldn't say it.

I didnt want to spoil the night. We watched Vin Diesel movie then there was a horror movie They Live in Us, in the beginning it was nice until the scary part, and now she was barried on my chest and this is exactly where I wanted her.

My heart started pounding hard and now it started by rubbing her hair. And she had beautiful silky long her. Now she started grinding my adulthood with her leg. That was a huge mistake as it aroused me and now I was carried away. The taste of her tongue was weird but her kiss was like she went for kissing lessons. The breathing was so emotional.

She grabbed my buttocks with her soft hands, I told myself now I will show her what my dad gave me. As soon we were done she told me to never tell anyone what we've done. Now this wasn't enough for me I wanted more than just sex.

She now told me she had twins and a boyfriend but he doesn't live with them. That was like a smack in the face. Now I wanted to back off but the connection we have, the intimacy we have was more stronger than my will.

She was as fit as an athlete, stubborn as a farmer, friendly as a nanny and deep down she had a heart so special. When I grow up my mother used to tell me if I want any girl to fall for me,l had to make her laugh. But every time Nicole laughed I was the one falling for her more and more. It is very hard to let go of anything that you have bond with but I heard to let go.

Well as we all know what goes around will always come around. So now karma is doing what he does best and firstly what started as a one night stands end up being all nights stands. What is wrong with me? Is that I am too lonely or I am just bored or I taking advantage of her or she is taking advantage of my week spot? Only God knows what caused the dog to only smile but not laugh out loud.

But as we all know we only live once right, so why not take the chance and just go with the flow. But wait what if now her boyfriend finds out is she gonna lose someone closer over this stupidity? Anyways it's not my fault I didnt let her so beautiful that even a blind can see. Thinking all this and to find out I was mumbling aloud to a point where one of my friends asked me if I was alright.

Its love that can only drive a man that crazy I guess. Now due to our circumstances we have to keep things under the carpet. Its either we together by me or together by her place to a point where her kids calls me uncle. We were all over ourselves those times lucky enough it never came to a point where one had to be caught out.

Now getting into this Situationship was walking in the park getting out was like chopping off your hands. One night changed my world forever. Only a single night, it made me pray harder. But God never answered my prayers. It's true. In one day, a life can change. Or more than one. Sometimes it's a single moment that alters everything in existence.

Sometimes it's the fall of dominoes, lined up in a pretty little row and designed so that each one will cause more and more pain. In a single day it's all changed, and there is no way to take it back. Those are the moments that defines you. As I stand outside the house I lived, two blocks from the shopping centre, the one night that made me who I am keeps on coming back to me. As hallucinate, and I hate flashbacks period.

But this didn't define my attitude nor my relationship with Nicole rather bring more good memories that we endowed throughout our time together. Now I wanted her for me and for me alone.

One thing that is adding to the challenges that we have nowadays is , selfishness. The reason why we fail to stand together is because we have so many people in our minds and we cant make a choice because we want all the beauty to ourselves. This is the biggest weakness we have as men. I will state this loudly; many of us never get education on how to make one choice and stick to it without seeing other choices better in one way or two. Please don't get me wrong,if you're married and happy don't think twice about your partner be fully committed cause they are snitches like us who are waiting for you to do her wrong and she will need a shoulder to cry on, then boom we snatch her.

After a long time of silent from both Nicole and I, I realized it was probably a sign to say move on with your life our SITUATIONSHIP was over. But little did I know it was just a wrong timing.

34

Social media platforms nowadays are the most common ways to communicate rather than older days things were not that complicated. It was so romantic to send your women a letter. It made everything much important when reading the letter. But unfortunately our generation has been colonized by new generation.

A message popped up on my phone while I was just sitting down thinking silently. I checked messages but couldn't get it only to find out it was from Facebook. Who might have sent me a message on Facebook? Curiosity hit my mind! And in a matter of seconds I was already reading the message. From far away you could see my face getting shiney, a little slower smile breaking loose, slowly becoming a big smile. And this girl had just made my day, it was Nicole.

Cherish every moment you got with your loved one, if there is an issue go fix it now before it's too late. Don't be like a selfish soccer player,who will fight to score a goal,ignoring the fact that he has a team that he can give the ball to and they can score so that the team wins and they all take th cup. Falling in love with someone is the easy part, the hard part is staying in love with one person forever.

Our situation continues to a point that I was deeply in love with her and she was in love with me, Weird part was that we both made a deal to never catch feelings just sex when one is in a bad situation that's all. But it never worked out that way even if you would try harder temptations were really.

Never give another man a chance to make your women happy. Regardless of what he do or did. There are words that were once spoken by a great leader and I consider these as words of wisdom. If today we were applying them most of us especially those in LOVE would be doing great things towards their partnership or relationship. "BIBLE" says I quote; " Ifyou're honest with the little,God will make you the Ruler of many". That alone, read it again and again until you understand the meaning of it and it is very important. Its simple as well that if you appreciate what you have God will reward you with more. Never think of another man if you already have one, never think of another woman if you already have one simple.

If there is anything you don't understand you can always ask to better yourself. *"A man who asks a question is a fool for a minute, But a man who does not ask is a fool for life"* CONFUCIUS, once said.

END
Dictionary

DATA FROM Oxford Languages[1]

POEM

MAMA (MOTHER)

mother

[ˈmʌðə]

NOUN

mother (noun) · mothers (plural noun) · Mother (noun) · Mother Superior (noun) · Reverend Mother (noun)

1. a woman in relation to her child or children:

"his mother was a painter" · "a mother of three" · "she returned to Bristol to nurse her ageing mother"

synonyms

female parent · biological mother · birth mother[2] · foster mother[3] · adoptive mother · stepmother[4] · surrogate

1. https://www.bing.com/ck/

a?!&&p=a6eb1572ec4bcbfbJmltdHM9MTY4MDA0ODAwMCZpZ3VpZD0yYWVlOWFlmOC1jOTU5LTYwODEtMzliMS04ODg0Yzgy YjYxYTAmaW5zaWQ9

NTU5OA&ptn=3&hsh=3&fclid=2aee9af8-c959-6081-39b1-

8884c82b61a0&psq=Mama+synonym&u=a1aHR0cDovL3d3dy5veGZvcmRkaWN0aW9uYXJpZXMuY29tLw&ntb=1

2. https://www.bing.com/ck/

a?!&&p=5aee18a277589d58JmltdHM9MTY4MDA0ODAwMCZpZ3VpZD0yYWVlOWVF

mOC1jOTU5LTYwODEtMzliMS04ODg0YzgyYjYxYTAmaW5zaWQ9NTYwNQ&ptn=3&

hsh=3&fclid=2aee9af8-c959-6081-39b1-

mother[5] · materfamilias[6] · matriarch[7] · Mata[8] · progenitress[9] · progenitrix

8884c82b61a0&u=a1L3NlYXJjaD9xPWRlZmluZStiaXJ0aCttb3RoZXImRk9STT1EQ1RSUVk&ntb=1

3. https://www.bing.com/ck/
a?!&&p=80d7b64fc9a60118JmltdHM9MTY4MDA0ODAwMCZpZ3VpZD0yYWVlOWFFmOC1jOTU5LTYwODEtMzliMS04ODg0YzgyYjYxYTAmaW5zaWQ9NTYwNg&ptn=3&hsh=3&fclid=2aee9af8-c959-6081-39b1-
8884c82b61a0&u=a1L3NlYXJjaD9xPWRlZmluZStmb3N0ZXIrbW90aGVyJkZPUk09RENUUlFZ&ntb=1

4. https://www.bing.com/ck/
a?!&&p=83d7d605d8aa3224JmltdHM9MTY4MDA0ODAwMCZpZ3VpZD0yYWVlOWVlOWFFmOC1jOTU5LTYwODEtMzliMS04ODg0YzgyYjYxYTAmaW5zaWQ9NTYwNw&ptn=3&hsh=3&fclid=2aee9af8-c959-6081-39b1-
8884c82b61a0&u=a1L3NlYXJjaD9xPWRlZmluZStzdGVwbW90aGVyJkZPUk09RENUUlFZ&ntb=1

5. https://www.bing.com/ck/
a?!&&p=667cc4bbf3010b2fJmltdHM9MTY4MDA0ODAwMCZpZ3VpZD0yYWVlOWFFmOC1jOTU5LTYwODEtMzliMS04ODg0YzgyYjYxYTAmaW5zaWQ9NTYwOA&ptn=3&hsh=3&fclid=2aee9af8-c959-6081-39b1-
8884c82b61a0&u=a1L3NlYXJjaD9xPWRlZmluZStzdXJyb2dhdGUrbW90aGVyJkZPUk09RENUUlFZ&ntb=1

6. https://www.bing.com/ck/
a?!&&p=684f6a8c6bdf155cJmltdHM9MTY4MDA0ODAwMCZpZ3VpZD0yYWVlOWFFmOC1jOTU5LTYwODEtMzliMS04ODg0YzgyYjYxYTAmaW5zaWQ9NTYwOQ&ptn=3&hsh=3&fclid=2aee9af8-c959-6081-39b1-
8884c82b61a0&u=a1L3NlYXJjaD9xPWRlZmluZSttYXRlcm5hbCZkZPUk09RENUUlFZ&ntb=1

7. https://www.bing.com/ck/
a?!&&p=2b4ef784415bd7b5JmltdHM9MTY4MDA0ODAwMCZpZ3VpZD0yYWVlOWFFmOC1jOTU5LTYwODEtMzliMS04ODg0YzgyYjYxYTAmaW5zaWQ9NTYxMA&ptn=3&hsh=3&fclid=2aee9af8-c959-6081-39b1-

- a female animal in relation to its offspring:

"a mother penguin"
synonyms
<u>dam</u>[10]

- *archaic*

(especially as a form of address) an elderly woman.

- an important female figure in the origin and early history of something:

8884c82b61a0&u=a1L3NlYXJjaD9xPWRlZmluZSttYXRyaWFyY2gmRk9STT1EQ1RSUVk&ntb=1

8. https://www.bing.com/ck/
a?!&&p=f07f2c891c24513dJmltdHM9MTY4MDA0ODAwMCZpZ3VpZD0yYWVlOWFmOC1jOTU5LTYwODEtMzliMS04ODg0YzgyYjYxYTAmaW5zaWQ9NTYxMQ&ptn=3&hsh=3&fclid=2aee9af8-c959-6081-39b1-8884c82b61a0&u=a1L3NlYXJjaD9xPWRlZmluZStNYXRhJkZPUk09RENUUlFZ&ntb=1

9. https://www.bing.com/ck/
a?!&&p=b803c8883d1cb589JmltdHM9MTY4MDA0ODAwMCZpZ3VpZD0yYWVlOWFmOC1jOTU5LTYwODEtMzliMS04ODg0YzgyYjYxYTAmaW5zaWQ9NTYxMg&ptn=3&hsh=3&fclid=2aee9af8-c959-6081-39b1-8884c82b61a0&u=a1L3NlYXJjaD9xPWRlZmluZStwcm9nZW5pdHJlc3MmRk9STT1EQ1RSUVk&ntb=1

10. https://www.bing.com/ck/
a?!&&p=607bf253a8259f82JmltdHM9MTY4MDA0ODAwMCZpZ3VpZD0yYWVlOWFmOC1jOTU5LTYwODEtMzliMS04ODg0YzgyYjYxYTAmaW5zaWQ9NTYxNg&ptn=3&hsh=3&fclid=2aee9af8-c959-6081-39b1-8884c82b61a0&u=a1L3NlYXJjaD9xPWRlZmluZStkYW0mRk9STT1EQ1RSUVk&ntb=1

"she will always be remembered as the mother of modern ecology" · "they are often referred to as the founding mothers of the Museum of Modern Art"

synonyms

originator[11] · initiator[12] · founder[13] · founding mother · inventor[14] · creator[15] · maker[16] · author[17] · prime mover[18] ·

11. https://www.bing.com/ck/
a?!&&p=a0b673f2cf746670JmltdHM9MTY4MDA0ODAwMCZpZ3VpZD0yYWVlOWFmOC1jOTU5LTYwODEtMzliMS04ODg0Yzgy YjYxYTAmaW5zaWQ9NTYyMg&ptn=3&hsh=3&fclid=2aee9af8-c959-6081-39b1-8884c82b61a0&u=a1L3NlYXJjaD9xPWRlZmluZStvcmlnaW5hW5hdG9yJkZPUk09RENRU1UlF Z&ntb=1

12. https://www.bing.com/ck/
a?!&&p=87e6e92abe74ef7fJmltdHM9MTY4MDA0ODAwMCZpZ3VpZD0yYWVlOWFmOC1jOTU5LTYwODEtMzliMS04ODg0Yzgy YjYxYTAmaW5zaWQ9NTYyMw&ptn=3&hsh=3&fclid=2aee9af8-c959-6081-39b1-8884c82b61a0&u=a1L3NlYXJjaD9xPWRlZmluZStpbml0aWF0b3ImRk9STT1EQ1RSUVk&ntb=1

13. https://www.bing.com/ck/
a?!&&p=814de42795ecf00fJmltdHM9MTY4MDA0ODAwMCZpZ3VpZD0yYWVlOWFmOC1jOTU5LTYwODEtMzliMS04ODg0Yzgy YjYxYTAmaW5zaWQ9NTYyNA&ptn=3&hsh=3&fclid=2aee9af8-c959-6081-39b1-8884c82b61a0&u=a1L3NlYXJjaD9xPWRlZmluZStmb3VuZGVyJkZPUk09RENRU1UlFZ&ntb=1

14. https://www.bing.com/ck/
a?!&&p=e797f34349deebd0JmltdHM9MTY4MDA0ODAwMCZpZ3VpZD0yYWVlOWFmOC1jOTU5LTYwODEtMzliMS04ODg0Yzgy YjYxYTAmaW5zaWQ9NTYyNQ&ptn=3&hsh=3&fclid=2aee9af8-c959-6081-39b1-8884c82b61a0&u=a1L3NlYXJjaD9xPWRlZmluZStpbnZlbnRvciZGT1JNPURDVFJRWQ&ntb=1

instigator[19] · architect[20] · engineer[21] · designer[22] · deviser[23] · planner[24] · contriver[25] · mastermind[26] · begetter[27]

15. https://www.bing.com/ck/
a?!&&p=3fdc4fbf701fc6c4JmltdHM9MTY4MDA0ODAwMCZpZ3VpZD0yYWVlOWFm
OC1jOTU5LTYwODEtMzliMS04ODg0YzgyYjYxYTAmaW5zaWQ9NTYyNg&ptn=3&hsh
=3&fclid=2aee9af8-c959-6081-39b1-
8884c82b61a0&u=a1L3NlYXJjaD9xPWRlZmluZStjcmVhdG9yJkZPUk09RENUUlFZ&nt
b=1

16. https://www.bing.com/ck/
a?!&&p=ef1b583c74e3c853JmltdHM9MTY4MDA0ODAwMCZpZ3VpZD0yYWVlOWFm
OC1jOTU5LTYwODEtMzliMS04ODg0YzgyYjYxYTAmaW5zaWQ9NTYyNw&ptn=3&hs
h=3&fclid=2aee9af8-c959-6081-39b1-
8884c82b61a0&u=a1L3NlYXJjaD9xPWRlZmluZSttYWtlciZGT1JNPURDVFJRWQ&ntb
=1

17. https://www.bing.com/ck/
a?!&&p=7a7e3ba132cd15f8JmltdHM9MTY4MDA0ODAwMCZpZ3VpZD0yYWVlOWFm
OC1jOTU5LTYwODEtMzliMS04ODg0YzgyYjYxYTAmaW5zaWQ9NTYyOA&ptn=3&hs
h=3&fclid=2aee9af8-c959-6081-39b1-
8884c82b61a0&u=a1L3NlYXJjaD9xPWRlZmluZSthdXRob3ImRk9STT1EQ1RSUVk&nt
b=1

18. https://www.bing.com/ck/
a?!&&p=9c10737aae413c66JmltdHM9MTY4MDA0ODAwMCZpZ3VpZD0yYWVlOWFm
OC1jOTU5LTYwODEtMzliMS04ODg0YzgyYjYxYTAmaW5zaWQ9NTYyOQ&ptn=3&hs
h=3&fclid=2aee9af8-c959-6081-39b1-
8884c82b61a0&u=a1L3NlYXJjaD9xPWRlZmluZStwcmltZSttb3ZlciZGT1JNPURDVFJR
WQ&ntb=1

19. https://www.bing.com/ck/
a?!&&p=8fd0b33e2c377dd5JmltdHM9MTY4MDA0ODAwMCZpZ3VpZD0yYWVlOWVlOWF
mOC1jOTU5LTYwODEtMzliMS04ODg0YzgyYjYxYTAmaW5zaWQ9NTYzMA&ptn=3&
hsh=3&fclid=2aee9af8-c959-6081-39b1-
8884c82b61a0&u=a1L3NlYXJjaD9xPWRlZmluZStpbnN0aWdhdG9yJkZPUk09RENUUl
FZ&ntb=1

41

20. https://www.bing.com/ck/
a?!&&p=de7f115e8999fcc1JmltdHM9MTY4MDA0ODAwMCZpZ3VpZD0yYWVlOWFm
OC1jOTU5LTYwODEtMzliMS04ODg0YzgyYjYxYTAmaW5zaWQ9NTYzMQ&ptn=3&hs
h=3&fclid=2aee9af8-c959-6081-39b1-
8884c82b61a0&u=a1L3NlYXJjaD9xPWRlZmluZSthcmNoaXRlY3QmRk9STT1EQ1RSU
Vk&ntb=1

21. https://www.bing.com/ck/
a?!&&p=644af00413778d16JmltdHM9MTY4MDA0ODAwMCZpZ3VpZD0yYWVlOWYF
mOC1jOTU5LTYwODEtMzliMS04ODg0YzgyYjYxYTAmaW5zaWQ9NTYzMg&ptn=3&h
sh=3&fclid=2aee9af8-c959-6081-39b1-
8884c82b61a0&u=a1L3NlYXJjaD9xPWRlZmluZStlbmdpbmVlciZGT1JNPURDVFJRWQ
&ntb=1

22. https://www.bing.com/ck/
a?!&&p=5872aae4e0d7465dJmltdHM9MTY4MDA0ODAwMCZpZ3VpZD0yYWVlOWYF
mOC1jOTU5LTYwODEtMzliMS04ODg0YzgyYjYxYTAmaW5zaWQ9NTYzMw&ptn=3&
hsh=3&fclid=2aee9af8-c959-6081-39b1-
8884c82b61a0&u=a1L3NlYXJjaD9xPWRlZmluZStkZXNpZ25lciZGT1JNPURDVFJRW
Q&ntb=1

23. https://www.bing.com/ck/
a?!&&p=5cdcd26a7ba0c3f1JmltdHM9MTY4MDA0ODAwMCZpZ3VpZD0yYWVlOWFm
OC1jOTU5LTYwODEtMzliMS04ODg0YzgyYjYxYTAmaW5zaWQ9NTYzNA&ptn=3&hs
h=3&fclid=2aee9af8-c959-6081-39b1-
8884c82b61a0&u=a1L3NlYXJjaD9xPWRlZmluZStkZXZic2VyZdPUk09RENUUlFZW&n
tb=1

24. https://www.bing.com/ck/
a?!&&p=32c3bbd1cd1bee7aJmltdHM9MTY4MDA0ODAwMCZpZ3VpZD0yYWVlOWYF
mOC1jOTU5LTYwODEtMzliMS04ODg0YzgyYjYxYTAmaW5zaWQ9NTYzNQ&ptn=3&
hsh=3&fclid=2aee9af8-c959-6081-39b1-
8884c82b61a0&u=a1L3NlYXJjaD9xPWRlZmluZStwbGFubmVyJkPUk09RENUUlFZW&n
tb=1

25. https://www.bing.com/ck/
a?!&&p=309e07fd83f52a08JmltdHM9MTY4MDA0ODAwMCZpZ3VpZD0yYWVlOWFm

- denoting an institution or organization from which others of the same type derive:

"the initiatives were based on the experience of the mother company"

- (especially as a title or form of address) the head of a female religious community.

1. NORTH AMERICAN

VERB
mother (verb) · mothers (third person present) · mothered (past tense) · mothered (past participle) · mothering (present participle)

1. bring up (a child) with care and affection:

OC1jOTU5LTYwODEtMzliMS04ODg0YzgyYjYxYTAmaW5zaWQ9NTYzNg&ptn=3&hsh=3&fclid=2aee9af8-c959-6081-39b1-8884c82b61a0&u=a1L3NlYXJjaD9xPWRlZmluZStjb250cml2ZXImRk9STT1EQ1RSSUVk&ntb=1

26. https://www.bing.com/ck/
a?!&&p=dec4a09fb5b3bf86JmltdHM9MTY4MDA0ODAwMCZpZ3VpZD0yYWVlOWFmOC1jOTU5LTYwODEtMzliMS04ODg0YzgyYjYxYTAmaW5zaWQ9NTYzNw&ptn=3&hsh=3&fclid=2aee9af8-c959-6081-39b1-8884c82b61a0&u=a1L3NlYXJjaD9xPWRlZmluZSttYXN0ZXJtaW5kJkZPUk09RENUUllF Z&ntb=1

27. https://www.bing.com/ck/
a?!&&p=73e4bb36b3b1f6e9JmltdHM9MTY4MDA0ODAwMCZpZ3VpZD0yYWVlOWFmOC1jOTU5LTYwODEtMzliMS04ODg0YzgyYjYxYTAmaW5zaWQ9NTYzOA&ptn=3&hsh=3&fclid=2aee9af8-c959-6081-39b1-8884c82b61a0&u=a1L3NlYXJjaD9xPWRlZmluZStiZWdldHRlciZGT1JNPURDVFJREWQ&ntb=1

"she didn't know how to mother my brother and he was very sensitive" · "he found a beautiful wife that mothered his children"

synonyms

bring up[28] · **care for** · **provide for** · **take care of**[29] · **attend to** · **look after**[30] · **rear**[31] · **support**[32] · **raise**[33] · **foster**[34] · **parent**[35] · **tend**[36] · **feed**[37] · **nourish**[38] · **provender**[39]

---

28. https://www.bing.com/ck/

a?!&&p=e3e878981fa07188JmltdHM9MTY4MDA0ODAwMCZpZ3VpZD0yYWVlOWFmOC1jOTU5LTYwODEtMzliMS04ODg0YzgyYjYxYTAmaW5zaWQ9NTY1MQ&ptn=3&hsh=3&fclid=2aee9af8-c959-6081-39b1-8884c82b61a0&u=a1L3NlYXJjaD9xPWRlZmluZZSticmluZyt1cCZGT1JNPURDVFJRWQ&ntb=1

29. https://www.bing.com/ck/

a?!&&p=021532c810d3066bJmltdHM9MTY4MDA0ODAwMCZpZ3VpZD0yYWVllOWFmOC1jOTU5LTYwODEtMzliMS04ODg0YzgyYjYxYTAmaW5zaWQ9NTY1Mg&ptn=3&hsh=3&fclid=2aee9af8-c959-6081-39b1-8884c82b61a0&u=a1L3NlYXJjaD9xPWRlZmluZZSt0YWtlK2NhcmUrb2YmRk9STT1EQ1RSUVk&ntb=1

30. https://www.bing.com/ck/

a?!&&p=65318b49c030c553JmltdHM9MTY4MDA0ODAwMCZpZ3VpZD0yYWVllOWFmOC1jOTU5LTYwODEtMzliMS04ODg0YzgyYjYxYTAmaW5zaWQ9NTY1Mw&ptn=3&hsh=3&fclid=2aee9af8-c959-6081-39b1-8884c82b61a0&u=a1L3NlYXJjaD9xPWRlZmluZZStsb29rK2FmdGVyJkZPUk09RENUUlF&Z&ntb=1

31. https://www.bing.com/ck/

a?!&&p=d2b90cbcdc263bfdJmltdHM9MTY4MDA0ODAwMCZpZ3VpZD0yYWVllOWFmOC1jOTU5LTYwODEtMzliMS04ODg0YzgyYjYxYTAmaW5zaWQ9NTY1NA&ptn=3&hsh=3&fclid=2aee9af8-c959-6081-39b1-8884c82b61a0&u=a1L3NlYXJjaD9xPWRlZmluZZStyZWFyJkZPUk09RENUUlFFZ&ntb=1

32. https://www.bing.com/ck/

a?!&&p=32d16d93efceb0b8JmltdHM9MTY4MDA0ODAwMCZpZ3VpZD0yYWVlOWFmOC1jOTU5LTYwODEtMzliMS04ODg0YzgyYjYxYTAmaW5zaWQ9NTY1NQ&ptn=3&hsh=3&fclid=2aee9af8-c959-6081-39b1-8884c82b61a0&u=a1L3NlYXJjaD9xPWRlZmluZZStzdXBwb3J0JkZPUk09RENUUlFFZ&ntb=1

33. https://www.bing.com/ck/

a?!&&p=0933672f7e7c446aJmltdHM9MTY4MDA0ODAwMCZpZ3VpZD0yYWVlOWFm OC1jOTU5LTYwODEtMzliMS04ODg0YzgyYjYxYTAmaW5zaWQ9NTY1Ng&ptn=3&hs h=3&fclid=2aee9af8-c959-6081-39b1- 8884c82b61a0&u=a1L3NlYXJjaD9xPWRlZmluZStyYWlzZSZGT1JNPURDVFJRWQ&nt b=1

34. https://www.bing.com/ck/

a?!&&p=f706d8df4825da99JmltdHM9MTY4MDA0ODAwMCZpZ3VpZD0yYWVlOWFm OC1jOTU5LTYwODEtMzliMS04ODg0YzgyYjYxYTAmaW5zaWQ9NTY1Nw&ptn=3&hs h=3&fclid=2aee9af8-c959-6081-39b1- 8884c82b61a0&u=a1L3NlYXJjaD9xPWRlZmluZStmb3N0ZXImRk9STT1EQ1RSUVk&n tb=1

35. https://www.bing.com/ck/

a?!&&p=775d260c7166f4cdJmltdHM9MTY4MDA0ODAwMCZpZ3VpZD0yYWVlOWFm OC1jOTU5LTYwODEtMzliMS04ODg0YzgyYjYxYTAmaW5zaWQ9NTY1OA&ptn=3&hs h=3&fclid=2aee9af8-c959-6081-39b1- 8884c82b61a0&u=a1L3NlYXJjaD9xPWRlZmluZStwYXJlbnQmRk9STT1EQ1RSUVk&nt b=1

36. https://www.bing.com/ck/

a?!&&p=ea07e414cbb238b0JmltdHM9MTY4MDA0ODAwMCZpZ3VpZD0yYWVlOWVlOWF mOC1jOTU5LTYwODEtMzliMS04ODg0YzgyYjYxYTAmaW5zaWQ9NTY1OQ&ptn=3& hsh=3&fclid=2aee9af8-c959-6081-39b1- 8884c82b61a0&u=a1L3NlYXJjaD9xPWRlZmluZSt0ZW5kJkZPUk09RENUUlFFFZ&ntb=1

37. https://www.bing.com/ck/

a?!&&p=587591a69df38128JmltdHM9MTY4MDA0ODAwMCZpZ3VpZD0yYWVlOWF mOC1jOTU5LTYwODEtMzliMS04ODg0YzgyYjYxYTAmaW5zaWQ9NTY2MA&ptn=3& hsh=3&fclid=2aee9af8-c959-6081-39b1- 8884c82b61a0&u=a1L3NlYXJjaD9xPWRlZmluZStmZWVkJkZPUk09RENUUlFFFZ&ntb= 1

38. https://www.bing.com/ck/

a?!&&p=3036e945ebbea95dJmltdHM9MTY4MDA0ODAwMCZpZ3VpZD0yYWVlOWF mOC1jOTU5LTYwODEtMzliMS04ODg0YzgyYjYxYTAmaW5zaWQ9NTY2MQ&ptn=3&

antonyms:

<u>neglect</u>[40]

- look after (someone) kindly and protectively, sometimes excessively so:

"she mothered her husband, insisting he should take cod liver oil in the winter"

synonyms

look after[41] · care for · take care of[42] · nurture[43] · nurse[44] · protect[45] · cherish[46] · tend[47] · raise[48] · rear[49] · pamper[50] ·

hsh=3&fclid=2aee9af8-c959-6081-39b1-8884c82b61a0&u=a1L3NlYXJjaD9xPWRlZmluaZStub3VyaXNoJkZPUk09RENUUlFZ&ntb=1

39. https://www.bing.com/ck/a?!&&p=d970ec937d7d1740JmltdHM9MTY4MDA0ODAwMCZpZ3VpZD0yYWVlOWFFmOC1jOTU5LTYwODEtMzliMS04ODg0YzgyYjYxYTAmaW5zaWQ9NTY2Mg&ptn=3&hsh=3&fclid=2aee9af8-c959-6081-39b1-8884c82b61a0&u=a1L3NlYXJjaD9xPWRlZmluaZStwcm92ZW5kZXXImRk9STT1EQ1RSU Vk&ntb=1

40. https://www.bing.com/ck/a?!&&p=6081912eadb9e536JmltdHM9MTY4MDA0ODAwMCZpZ3VpZD0yYWVlOWFFmOC1jOTU5LTYwODEtMzliMS04ODg0YzgyYjYxYTAmaW5zaWQ9NTY2NA&ptn=3&hsh=3&fclid=2aee9af8-c959-6081-39b1-8884c82b61a0&u=a1L3NlYXJjaD9xPWRlZmluaZStuZWdsZWN0JkZPUk09RENUUlFZ&ntb=1

41. https://www.bing.com/ck/a?!&&p=f23efd03a7ee5b72JmltdHM9MTY4MDA0ODAwMCZpZ3VpZD0yYWVlOWFFmOC1jOTU5LTYwODEtMzliMS04ODg0YzgyYjYxYTAmaW5zaWQ9NTY2Nw&ptn=3&hsh=3&fclid=2aee9af8-c959-6081-39b1-

8884c82b61a0&u=a1L3NlYXJjaD9xPWRlZmluZStsb29rK2FmdGVyJkZPUk09RENUUlF Z&ntb=1

42. https://www.bing.com/ck/
a?!&&p=081f10a9469ec094JmltdHM9MTY4MDA0ODAwMCZpZ3VpZD0yYWVlOWFm OC1jOTU5LTYwODEtMzliMS04ODg0YzgyYjYxYTAmaW5zaWQ9NTY2OA&ptn=3&hs h=3&fclid=2aee9af8-c959-6081-39b1-
8884c82b61a0&u=a1L3NlYXJjaD9xPWRlZmluZSt0YWdlK2NhcmUrb2YmRk9STT1EQ1 RSUVk&ntb=1

43. https://www.bing.com/ck/
a?!&&p=ba80da05e3f0eea2JmltdHM9MTY4MDA0ODAwMCZpZ3VpZD0yYWVlOWFm OC1jOTU5LTYwODEtMzliMS04ODg0YzgyYjYxYTAmaW5zaWQ9NTY2OQ&ptn=3&hs h=3&fclid=2aee9af8-c959-6081-39b1-
8884c82b61a0&u=a1L3NlYXJjaD9xPWRlZmluZStudXJ0dXJlJkZPUk09RENUUlFZ&nt b=1

44. https://www.bing.com/ck/
a?!&&p=c5bbe54e4f848896JmltdHM9MTY4MDA0ODAwMCZpZ3VpZD0yYWVlOWFm OC1jOTU5LTYwODEtMzliMS04ODg0YzgyYjYxYTAmaW5zaWQ9NTY3MA&ptn=3&hs h=3&fclid=2aee9af8-c959-6081-39b1-
8884c82b61a0&u=a1L3NlYXJjaD9xPWRlZmluZStudXJzZSZGT1JNPURDVFJRWQ&nt b=1

45. https://www.bing.com/ck/
a?!&&p=aae1083828d96029JmltdHM9MTY4MDA0ODAwMCZpZ3VpZD0yYWVlOWF mOC1jOTU5LTYwODEtMzliMS04ODg0YzgyYjYxYTAmaW5zaWQ9NTY3MQ&ptn=3& hsh=3&fclid=2aee9af8-c959-6081-39b1-
8884c82b61a0&u=a1L3NlYXJjaD9xPWRlZmluZStwcm90ZWN0JkZPUk09RENUUlFZ& ntb=1

46. https://www.bing.com/ck/
a?!&&p=f1ecd572ff26cc57JmltdHM9MTY4MDA0ODAwMCZpZ3VpZD0yYWVlOWFm OC1jOTU5LTYwODEtMzliMS04ODg0YzgyYjYxYTAmaW5zaWQ9NTY3Mg&ptn=3&hs h=3&fclid=2aee9af8-c959-6081-39b1-
8884c82b61a0&u=a1L3NlYXJjaD9xPWRlZmluZStjaGVyaXNoJkZPUk09RENUUlFZ&nt b=1

48

47. https://www.bing.com/ck/

a?!&&p=182b1426e43da5b4JmltdHM9MTY4MDA0ODAwMCZpZ3VpZD0yYWVlOWF mOC1jOTU5LTYwODEtMzliMS04ODg0YzgyYjYxYTAmaW5zaWQ9NTY3Mw&ptn=3& hsh=3&fclid=2aee9af8-c959-6081-39b1-

8884c82b61a0&u=a1L3NlYXJjaD9xPWRlZmluZSt0ZW5kJkZPUk09RENUUlFZ&ntb=1

48. https://www.bing.com/ck/

a?!&&p=0d774c616854cbd7JmltdHM9MTY4MDA0ODAwMCZpZ3VpZD0yYWVlOWF mOC1jOTU5LTYwODEtMzliMS04ODg0YzgyYjYxYTAmaW5zaWQ9NTY3NA&ptn=3& hsh=3&fclid=2aee9af8-c959-6081-39b1-

8884c82b61a0&u=a1L3NlYXJjaD9xPWRlZmluZStyYWlzZSZGT1JNPURDVFJRWQ&nt b=1

49. https://www.bing.com/ck/

a?!&&p=9730bf24d2dd1ab8JmltdHM9MTY4MDA0ODAwMCZpZ3VpZD0yYWVlOWF mOC1jOTU5LTYwODEtMzliMS04ODg0YzgyYjYxYTAmaW5zaWQ9NTY3NQ&ptn=3& hsh=3&fclid=2aee9af8-c959-6081-39b1-

8884c82b61a0&u=a1L3NlYXJjaD9xPWRlZmluZStyZWFyJkZPUk09RENUUlFZ&ntb=1

50. https://www.bing.com/ck/

a?!&&p=f9d66cd165098ed1JmltdHM9MTY4MDA0ODAwMCZpZ3VpZD0yYWVlOWF mOC1jOTU5LTYwODEtMzliMS04ODg0YzgyYjYxYTAmaW5zaWQ9NTY3Ng&ptn=3&h sh=3&fclid=2aee9af8-c959-6081-39b1-

8884c82b61a0&u=a1L3NlYXJjaD9xPWRlZmluZStwYW1wZXImRk9STT1EQ1RSUVk& ntb=1

coddle[51] · **cosset**[52] · **baby**[53] · **overprotect**[54] · **overparent**[55] · **fuss over** · **indulge**[56] · **spoil**[57]

---

51. https://www.bing.com/ck/
a?!&&p=e92913e74e2b8c32JmltdHM9MTY4MDA0ODAwMCZpZ3VpZD0yYWVlOWF
mOC1jOTU5LTYwODEtMzliMS04ODg0YzgyYjYxYTAmaW5zaWQ9NTY3Nw&ptn=3&
hsh=3&fclid=2aee9af8-c959-6081-39b1-
8884c82b61a0&u=a1L3NlYXJjaD9xPWRlZmluZStjb2RkbGUmRk9STT1EQ1RSUVk&nt
b=1

52. https://www.bing.com/ck/
a?!&&p=329d57a5384c7cfaJmltdHM9MTY4MDA0ODAwMCZpZ3VpZD0yYWVlOWFm
OC1jOTU5LTYwODEtMzliMS04ODg0YzgyYjYxYTAmaW5zaWQ9NTY3OA&ptn=3&hs
h=3&fclid=2aee9af8-c959-6081-39b1-
8884c82b61a0&u=a1L3NlYXJjaD9xPWRlZmluZStjb3NzZXQmRk9STT1EQ1RSUVk&n
tb=1

53. https://www.bing.com/ck/
a?!&&p=0e5b6b5f977708abJmltdHM9MTY4MDA0ODAwMCZpZ3VpZD0yYWVlOWFm
OC1jOTU5LTYwODEtMzliMS04ODg0YzgyYjYxYTAmaW5zaWQ9NTY3OQ&ptn=3&hs
h=3&fclid=2aee9af8-c959-6081-39b1-
8884c82b61a0&u=a1L3NlYXJjaD9xPWRlZmluZStiYWJ5JkZPUk09RENUUllFZ&ntb=1

54. https://www.bing.com/ck/
a?!&&p=e044cf8218111d76JmltdHM9MTY4MDA0ODAwMCZpZ3VpZD0yYWVlOWFm
OC1jOTU5LTYwODEtMzliMS04ODg0YzgyYjYxYTAmaW5zaWQ9NTY4MA&ptn=3&hs
h=3&fclid=2aee9af8-c959-6081-39b1-
8884c82b61a0&u=a1L3NlYXJjaD9xPWRlZmluZStvdmVycHJvdGVjdCZGT1JNPURDVF
JRWQ&ntb=1

55. https://www.bing.com/ck/
a?!&&p=248cc818c35f4a6bJmltdHM9MTY4MDA0ODAwMCZpZ3VpZD0yYWVlOWFm
OC1jOTU5LTYwODEtMzliMS04ODg0YzgyYjYxYTAmaW5zaWQ9NTY4MQ&ptn=3&hs
h=3&fclid=2aee9af8-c959-6081-39b1-
8884c82b61a0&u=a1L3NlYXJjaD9xPWRlZmluZStvdmVycGFyZW50JkZPUk09RENUUl
FZ&ntb=1

antonyms:

<u>neglect</u>[58]

1. dated

give birth to:

"she's mothered two foals that have gone on to be impressive dressage competitors"

synonyms

give birth to · have[59] · deliver[60] · bear[61] · produce[62] · bring forth[63] · birth[64] · be brought to bed of

56. https://www.bing.com/ck/

a?!&&p=66245c11f99cc14aJmltdHM9MTY4MDA0ODAwMCZpZ3VpZD0yYWVlOWFmOC1jOTU5LTYwODEtMzliMS04ODg0YzgyYjYxYTAmaW5zaWQ9NTY4Mg&ptn=3&hsh=3&fclid=2aee9af8-c959-6081-39b1-8884c82b61a0&u=a1L3NlYXJjaD9xPWRlZmluZStpbmR1bGdlJkZPUk09RENUUlFZ&ntb=1

57. https://www.bing.com/ck/

a?!&&p=ef301331a938d9e6JmltdHM9MTY4MDA0ODAwMCZpZ3VpZD0yYWVlOWFmOC1jOTU5LTYwODEtMzliMS04ODg0YzgyYjYxYTAmaW5zaWQ9NTY4Mw&ptn=3&hsh=3&fclid=2aee9af8-c959-6081-39b1-8884c82b61a0&u=a1L3NlYXJjaD9xPWRlZmluZStzcG9pbCZGT1JNPURDVFJRWQ&ntb=1

58. https://www.bing.com/ck/

a?!&&p=3f882151768331d8JmltdHM9MTY4MDA0ODAwMCZpZ3VpZD0yYWVlOWFmOC1jOTU5LTYwODEtMzliMS04ODg0YzgyYjYxYTAmaW5zaWQ9NTY4NQ&ptn=3&hsh=3&fclid=2aee9af8-c959-6081-39b1-8884c82b61a0&u=a1L3NlYXJjaD9xPWRlZmluZStuZWdsZWN0JkZPUk09RENUUlFZ&ntb=1

59. https://www.bing.com/ck/
a?!&&p=2fd34626f9f88d69JmltdHM9MTY4MDA0ODAwMCZpZ3VpZD0yYWVlOWFm
OC1jOTU5LTYwODEtMzliMS04ODg0YzgyYjYxYTAmaW5zaWQ9NTY4OA&ptn=3&hs
h=3&fclid=2aee9af8-c959-6081-39b1-
8884c82b61a0&u=a1L3NlYXJjaD9xPWRlZmluZStoYXZllJkZPUk09RENUUlFZ&ntb=1

60. https://www.bing.com/ck/
a?!&&p=49f34f7700356846JmltdHM9MTY4MDA0ODAwMCZpZ3VpZD0yYWVlOWFm
OC1jOTU5LTYwODEtMzliMS04ODg0YzgyYjYxYTAmaW5zaWQ9NTY4OQ&ptn=3&hs
h=3&fclid=2aee9af8-c959-6081-39b1-
8884c82b61a0&u=a1L3NlYXJjaD9xPWRlZmluZStkZWxpdmVyJkZPUk09RENUUlFZ&n
tb=1

61. https://www.bing.com/ck/
a?!&&p=0815e0a4fac1127aJmltdHM9MTY4MDA0ODAwMCZpZ3VpZD0yYWVlOWFm
OC1jOTU5LTYwODEtMzliMS04ODg0YzgyYjYxYTAmaW5zaWQ9NTY5MA&ptn=3&hs
h=3&fclid=2aee9af8-c959-6081-39b1-
8884c82b61a0&u=a1L3NlYXJjaD9xPWRlZmluZStiZWFyJkZPUk09RENUUlFZ&ntb=1

62. https://www.bing.com/ck/
a?!&&p=486d42e74dc910fcJmltdHM9MTY4MDA0ODAwMCZpZ3VpZD0yYWVlOWFm
OC1jOTU5LTYwODEtMzliMS04ODg0YzgyYjYxYTAmaW5zaWQ9NTY5MQ&ptn=3&hs
h=3&fclid=2aee9af8-c959-6081-39b1-
8884c82b61a0&u=a1L3NlYXJjaD9xPWRlZmluZStwcm9kdWNlJkZPUk09RENUUlFZ&
ntb=1

63. https://www.bing.com/ck/
a?!&&p=ae633f377c414c79JmltdHM9MTY4MDA0ODAwMCZpZ3VpZD0yYWVlOWFm
OC1jOTU5LTYwODEtMzliMS04ODg0YzgyYjYxYTAmaW5zaWQ9NTY5Mg&ptn=3&hs
h=3&fclid=2aee9af8-c959-6081-39b1-
8884c82b61a0&u=a1L3NlYXJjaD9xPWRlZmluZSticmluZytmb3J0aCZGT1JNPURDVFJ
RWQ&ntb=1

64. https://www.bing.com/ck/
a?!&&p=7f8f02b6f2fbf010JmltdHM9MTY4MDA0ODAwMCZpZ3VpZD0yYWVlOWVm
OC1jOTU5LTYwODEtMzliMS04ODg0YzgyYjYxYTAmaW5zaWQ9NTY5Mw&ptn=3&hs
h=3&fclid=2aee9af8-c959-6081-39b1-

ORIGIN

Old English mōdor, of Germanic origin; related to Dutch moeder and German Mutter, from an Indo-European root shared by Latin mater and Greek mētēr.

TO ALL WOMEN !!

Mama you're my heartbeat
Mama you're my blood flow.
Mama you're my everything.
When the house breaks you fix it.
When the house is empty, you fill it
But yet all your children have lost their respect for you.
When you cry, we all cry
When the home has hate, you bring love.
When the man and children are hungry you feed them.
When there is no water in the house you go fetch it.
When there is cold in the house you bring warmth.
Oh Mama, yet your children have forgotten you.
Mama!Mama!Mama!

You change sadness into happiness.
You change hate into love.
You change anger into smiles.
You love deeply.
You care deeply.
You inspire deeply.
You encourage deeply.
You motivate deeply.
You are a Wonder Woman
There is no person stronger, wiser, or more dedicated

8884c82b61a0&u=a1L3NlYXJjaD9xPWRlZmluaZStiaXJ0aCZGT1JNPURDVFJRWQ&nt
b=1

Than a mother.
MOM, you are the reflection of WOW.
Mom, you're a wonderful mother,
So gentle, yet so strong.
The many ways you show you care
Always make me feel I belong.
You're patient when I'm foolish;
You give guidance when I ask;
It seems you can do most anything;
You're the master of every task.
I love you more than you know;
You have my total respect.
If I had my choice of mothers,
You'd be the one I'd select!
Since the day I was small
Till the day I became tall
Since I began understanding things
Till the day I got my own wings
Your love has never fallen short
You have been my only support
I want to hold you tight and hug you
I just want to say thank you.
Mom you're the greatest, Mom you're the best,
You put up with all of us, we're real pests
You feed us, help us, and always are there,
We thought we give you this "love you" card, just to be fair
When the going gets tough,
And the days are rough
I know that you'll always be there,
You'll help me in every affair.
I appreciate all that you do,
I hope I can be a good mother like you

You can see it in their eyes,
in tender hugs and long good-byes,
a love that only moms and daughters know.
You can see it in their smiles,
through passing years and changing styles,
a friendship that continually seems to grow.
You can see it in their lives,
the joy each one of them derives,
in just knowing that the other one is there...
To care and to understand,
lend an ear or hold a hand,
and to celebrate the memories they share.
My Mother, my friend so dear
throughout my life you're always near.
A tender smile to guide my way
You're the sunshine to light my day.
Sisters are nice, brothers are too,
Daddies are nice, and help me pull through
But mothers are the real heroes to me,
They help me and love me,
My mother's my friend and cheerleader, don't you see?
I know how often I took you for granted
when I was growing up.
I always assumed you'd be there
when I needed you...
and you always were.
But I never really thought about what that meant
till I got older and began to realize
how often your time and energy were devoted to me.
so now, for all the times I didn't say it before,
thank you, Mom...I love you so very much!
Mom, I wish I had words to tell

How much you mean to me.
I am the person I am today,
Because you let me be.
Your unconditional love
Made me happy, strong, secure.
Your teaching and example
Made me confident, mature.
In all the world, there is no mother
Better than my own.
You're the best and wisest person, Mom
I have ever known

There is no blessing
quite so dear...
as a mom like you
to love year after year.
I know you were there when I took my first breath.
You supported my first steps and dried all my tears.
You loved me despite my flaws and that is so true,
Nothing can take away the love between me and you.
You are my mother and that is just fine because nothing can
separate us even the end of all time.

For a special mom on this special day,
Your daughter has some words that she wants to say
Please know that I appreciate all the things that you do
Love you so much, Mom, happy Mother's Day to you!
Just one little wish for you, Mom,
But it's loving and happy and true-
It's a wish that the nicest and best things
Will always keep coming to you!
I love you to the moon and back
To infinity and beyond
I love you so much, I didn't sneak out that one time I really
wanted to
I love you so very much, I deal with my siblings
My mom, my confidant, and my very best friend
You know me better than I know myself
I don't know what I would do without you,
I would be lost
I think you should know, you mean more to me than any
poem could ever show

Oh, forgive us MAMA!!
Grateful and Gratitude's for your works!!!!!

** THANK YOU.**

End

ABOUT: *Pinel Motswagole grew up as an only child. Since both his parents didn't have any siblings either, Pinel also grew up as an only grandchild. He grew up in a small town on the outskirt of Polokwane in a village called Moletjie, Ga-Ngoasheng with adults—his parents and grandparents. Because of this, he never really knew what it meant to be a kid. Since the adults around Pinel were quite abusive, he didn't learn how to relate well with other kids. Growing up, Pinel felt accustomed to the company of adults. He was always more mature than the other children at school.*

Even when he gained friends, he often felt annoyed at them while growing up because he felt that they were too childish. The adults who raised Pinel had not invested a lot in him this encouraged him to excel in all of his subjects as well as any hobbies he decided to take up. Now that he's all grown up, accepts that back then, he may have seemed smug to his peers. While he didn't realize this back then, he hadn't learned self-awareness until years later. When Pinel was in high school, he started feeling the pressure from his parents' and grandparents' high expectations. Gradually, he stopped joining extra-curricular activities and instead, made the choice to work. Still Pinel finished at the top of his class, although he wasn't the valedictorian. Looking back, Pinel thinks that he didn't try as hard because he didn't want to give his family the satisfaction. He also worked to pay his bills and, after several jobs, he started working for an investment firm.

From there, he aimed to meet his potential, take on new challenges, but he didn't strive hard to go beyond expectations. Probably because of the kind of family he grew up in, Pinel never imagined himself having a family of his own. He didn't want to get tied down by a wife and children, so he always believed that marriage wasn't for him. Even though he never learned how to be a kid, he's hoping his little bundle of joy will teach him the joys of childhood when the time comes. This is where he gets his strength and motivation.

Don't miss out!

Visit the website below and you can sign up to receive emails whenever Pinel Motswagole publishes a new book. There's no charge and no obligation.

https://books2read.com/r/B-A-SARX-HPIHC

BOOKS 2 READ

Connecting independent readers to independent writers.